MY PASSIONATE MOTHER

MY
PASSIONATE
MOTHER

a novel

JUDY FEIFFER

RANDOM HOUSE
NEW YORK

All rights reserved under International and Pan-American
Copyright Conventions. Published in the United States by
Random House, an imprint of The Random House Publishing Group,
a division of Random House, Inc., New York, and simultaneously
in Canada by Random House of Canada Limited, Toronto.

RANDOM HOUSE and colophon are
registered trademarks of Random House, Inc.

LIBRARY OF CONGRESS CATALOGING-IN-PUBLICATION DATA
Feiffer, Judy.
My passionate mother: a novel / Judy Feiffer.
p. cm.
ISBN 1-4000-6220-9
1. Triangles (Interpersonal relations)—Fiction. 2. Mothers
and daughters—Fiction. 3. Women—New England—Fiction.
4. Loss (Psychology)—Fiction. 5. Male friendship—Fiction.
6. New England—Fiction. 7. Islands—Fiction. I. Title.
PS3556.E419M9 2004
813'.54—dc22   2003058624

Printed in the United States of America on acid-free paper

Random House website address: www.atrandom.com

246897531

FIRST EDITION

Book design by Casey Hampton

TO KATE, CHRIS, AND MADDY

MY PASSIONATE MOTHER

IT'S AS IF IT NEVER HAPPENED BEFORE.

Me, Joely, watching the ferry glide into the slip, not seeing him but knowing he's on deck, that he looks toward shore, a hint of laughter in his slate-gray eyes, engaging you, drawing you in, telling you he understands without saying a word.

There goes the whistle, a sharp hard blast followed by two short ones.

Now I see him, taller than the others. I know he is nervous, knowing I wait as Claire once waited, my impatient excited mother who held my hand, released it to lift a camera to her eye, click click clicking until she got it right, the exact smile or expression she would develop, enlarge, and hide in her secret cache.

And when she was off island and I was alone, I would go into her files and search, not for the photographs taken for publication, but for those for her eyes only, pictures of his torso, his shoulders and legs. And in those moments, alone with Claire's secret, I did not question if I was violating her trust, I simply felt free to love him without a daughter's shame.

Sometimes there was a new photograph and sometimes one was missing. I knew she had it with her, that when she returned, she would replace it in its plastic sleeve and think she was safe.

Now he sees me and breaks free of the other passengers. He carries a briefcase and computer. His suitcase, on a gurney, is wheeled to the street. A boyhood friend who works for the steamship authority calls his name and Joe stops for a moment of talk. Then he walks down the jetty and onto the wharf.

And it's the same; it's almost the same.

Shadows lengthening in the afternoon sun, the cries of circling gulls, a splatter of sea foam against the wooden piles, the belted raincoat he wears like a uniform.

Yes, almost the same. Yet, nothing's the same, for it's not Claire who waits but me, breathless as I watch his long graceful stride and wonder if love is genetic, transmitted prenatally, like a craving for alcohol or drugs; and what does it matter, this hunger inside me, for Joe has come home and is standing beside me, his warm low voice saying, "It's a shock to see you looking like that little girl who used to wait beside her mother."

"Let's get your things," I say and ignore the remark.

He pulls a suitcase from the gurney and we get into my car. We pass a weathered bronze statue, a monument to the men lost at sea, and I turn onto Water Street with its French café and seafood restaurant, movie house with a garish red poster, and the Pequod Emporium with a bright neon sign.

"Notice the changes?"

"Places don't change. We freshen them up with a coat of paint or they rot in decay, but they're only brick and mortar."

"Then what does change?"

"People."

"You mean you and me?"

"I mean summer folk who come with consumer hopes, expectations of happiness, as if happiness is a promissory note and summer's the season to redeem it, but they're gone by Labor Day, and Pequod's ours and life is normal."

"Normal! What's that?"

Joe laughs. My God, the man is handsome.

"Why, normal's the coming of fall, trees turning a fiery red, a wind blowing up the sea. It's the hum of the quahog boats, the clink of bottles as the milkman makes his rounds, footsteps on a lonely street."

5

Joe pauses. "Normal's one day following another without dramatic upheaval or event," he says.

"Sounds too good to be real."

"Why, you little skeptic. All right, Joely, you tell me. What's normal?"

"I think normal is when all the passion we've hidden away and buried goes wild inside us and explodes."

I know he listens, that he struggles with what Claire once called his inner code of honor, and I wonder if people do change, or am I fated, a child of fate, helpless against a dark desire that is my mother's legacy.

My MOTHER ALWAYS HAD TWO MEN: MY FATHER, FINN, who was her husband, and Finn's cousin and best friend, Joe, who was my mother's lover. And if Claire didn't love them both, both Finn and Joe Hurley loved her.

No one talked of the danger or consequences of the way we lived. Before her marriage to Finn, the men had agreed on sharing her, and I accepted it as normal.

Once, it was the island scandal, but with time, the rumors stretched out like an old rubber band, and now everyone accepted it. No one seemed to care, or if they did, they spoke of us in whispers.

Everyone but Claire, who only wanted to talk.

"It's important you understand," she used to tell me. "The three of us and how we live was Finn's idea. What he wanted. So you see, Joely, I've got Daddy's complete approval."

Since I was a child, I accepted the fact that I was Claire's captive audience, the vessel through which she relieved herself of guilt, that there wasn't enough love in the world to protect my mother from herself, or the way she loved. She made me feel that only I could save her, so she bore her soul, tore the pain from her heart, and I gave myself up to Claire's confession, and our illusion of intimacy, a daughter sharing her mother's secret life.

And I've often wondered if my loving Joe wasn't sown in me like a little seed, watered by my mother's tears until it burst into bloom. From my earliest years, I felt the force of Claire's passion, bending, twisting, and shaping my life.

And young as I was, I knew what was happening would be the story of our lives. If I loved Joe, he was hers; from the beginning Joe belonged to my mother. And so we lived: Finn, Joe, Claire, and me, and it seemed to work, our tangled web of lust and love, and then, one day, it all went bust.

Pequod is twenty miles long, fifteen miles wide, and shaped like a half-moon. Composed of a half dozen small towns, we have farms for produce, meadows for grazing, an ocean famous for fishing, and silky soft beaches that snake along the southern shore. Rumor has it Herman Melville, the author of *Moby-Dick,* visited the island, and under the spell of the rolling hills, the high timbered oaks, and the great gray cliffs overlooking the sea, wrote in his journal, "I shall call Ahab's poor battered ship *The Pequod.*"

Our winters are harsh and often brutal. Towns shut down, the landscape is barren. Heavy snows turn into sheets of ice, torrential rains are followed by a thaw, and suddenly, the air is crystal clear. Bursts of sunlight fall through the treetops onto the streets, and there's an explosion of hyacinth, daffodil, and flowering dogwood. Town house porticos are scrubbed bright and white, farmhouse doors are unbolted, and everyone rushes out to greet a neighbor, free, at last, of a long winter cocoon.

At the northern end of the island, bay and ocean intercept, and a low rocky coastline flattens into a meadow, bare except for a knotty old oak. My mother loved this weathered tree. She called it a friend and wrapped her arms around its trunk. I asked her why she loved it so, and she said, "It's my soul mate. I sit under the branches and look at the sea, watch the waves swell and collapse, become a part of the undertow, and I am one with it, all of it, I am the sea and the sea is me. I lean against my trusted old friend, tell it my secrets, and under its branches, luck is with me and I am safe."

On one side of the tree, the ocean pounds against the cliffs, and on the other side, a path slopes toward the bay with only a stump, a stone, or a low-lying bush in its path. Then it smooths out, flat and perpendicular, and falls into the water.

Children love to come and play. At high tide, they climb on the rocks and watch the crashing waves, and when the tide is low, they take mud baths, catch crabs and sea anemones. They drape themselves with strands of seaweed, dancing with seaweed, a favorite sport.

◌◌◌

W E LIVE ON AN ISLAND, RISING OUT OF THE SEA, AND man, his boat, and the sea are one, intertwined and inter-dependent, man dependent on the sea to bring food and life to the island, the sea taking it away, or unto itself, swallowing it whole, as it did my mother's father when she was a child.

As far back as is known, the men in Claire's line were fishing men. Chasing a whale, being chased by a whale, tracking it into the treacherous currents of the Atlantic, Pacific, or the shifting shoals of the ice-bound Arctic Sea. Men were away from home for three or more years, placed in irons or punished by the lash for an infraction of the rules. It was a perilous life, but in the nineteenth century, a young man living on an island had limited choices. Whaling was a way to make a decent living and how a

9

young man advanced himself. But the dangers and hazards of the great whale hunt convinced my great-great-grandfather to break with family tradition.

No one is certain how he came to photography or where he learned his craft, but the Pequod Historical Society lists the date as in the early 1860s.

Photography was about twenty-five years old. The North was pitted against the South in a brutal civil war. My great-great-grandfather had seen the harrowing pictures of carnage and destruction made by Mathew Brady and the brave men who lugged their heavy eight-by-ten cameras from battlefield to battlefield, and he was determined to join their ranks. So, leaving a wife and young son behind, he connected with the men who photographed the horrors. At Antietam, a bullet shattered his leg. My great-great-grandfather recuperated in a military hospital and came back to Pequod to live.

A one-legged war casualty, he set up a photography shop on Main Street. When his son was old enough to learn, he brought him into the business. His son taught his son, my grandfather, who photographed the ships, a hurricane that ripped apart the island, made stereoscopic views, *cartes de visite,* and portraits of visiting celebrities, like President Franklin D. Roosevelt. Grampa proudly hung the portrait in the window of his shop, and there it stayed until his death.

My grandfather was an old-fashioned romantic who longed to recapture the adventures of his forefathers. He heard a refurbished vessel was sailing to the Arctic to reenact the voyage of a whaling ship, and he signed on as photographer. And that was the fateful irony, that the vessel didn't explode on a faraway shore, but a mile outside of Pequod. A sudden burst of flame, a sheet of fire, millions of sparks, acrid smoke turning the sky soiled and gray, another explosion, and another, and the sea opened up to swallow ship and cargo. The only remains were bodies clinging to wood or pieces of debris.

My grandfather's body was among those recovered. He was brought back to Pequod and buried in the old Seaman's Cemetery, on a hillock overlooking the bay.

Like the heroine of a New England ghost story, my grandmother threw herself upon her husband's grave. She prayed for his ghost to appear so she could reclaim him, but his ghost never materialized, and my grandmother's hopes grew cold and dim, her only solace in a bottle of gin. And there you would find her, in the sod and the dark, sprawled upon his tombstone, a poor pathetic drunk, crying over the loss of the good times, which, according to my mother, were never very good.

My grandmother was destitute, a penniless widow living off a small insurance policy that was soon consumed by liquor, so it fell to my mother to forage for the money they would need to survive.

Claire was young, quick-witted, and pretty. Using her great good looks, smiling a beckoning smile, she sang and danced on the sidewalks of Pequod for change or, on a lucky day, dollars from sympathetic passersby.

She enjoyed disguising her sex, her red hair tucked under a cap, her lithe body hidden in boy's clothing, and found the androgynous switch from girl to boy and back to girl was a lure in greasing the pockets of her public. She sang, danced, and strutted, and those who gave a dollar on Monday returned on Tuesday and gave her another.

In the beginning, Claire seemed unaware of her mysterious power, but she soon began to realize how attractive she was to men. It was like a secret gift and she delighted in using it, not only to make money, but because it excited her. She was like a gambler tempting fate, becoming habituated to admiration and applause.

Claire also scavenged the town dump—the dumptique, she called it—with its variety of treasures, men's and women's old clothes, children's castoffs, furniture and kitchen equipment, a half-used lipstick or bottle of cologne, discarded spoils she was delighted to find.

At first it was a struggle, the smiling and pretending, but after a while she perfected the art of it, and pretense became a second skin.

So one way or another, Claire and her drunken dependent mother endured the hardship and privation. It was useless to worry about tomorrow. All that mattered was getting the best from today.

My PATERNAL GRANDFATHER FOUNDED THE *PEQUOD Post,* a weekly newspaper serving the island and read by summer residents and subscribers who wanted the news year-round.

My father, Finn, worked on the paper weekends and vacations. On graduating high school, he became the managing editor.

When his father died, Finn took over as publisher and editor in chief. He worked a seven-day week, often into the night, and said, "I've grown up with the smell of printer's ink. It's a part of my nervous system."

Finn loved the paper and was patient with the old machines. When one grew odd or cranky, the way an old press is prone to do, he tinkered with it, ministered like a country doctor with an ailing prima donna. "You're my high-strung, nervous beauty," he'd purr, "but you're the only one I've got, and I need you strong and healthy."

This was Finn's life, the island folk streaming into the office knowing he would open his wise, sympathetic heart to whoever needed him. It seemed to Finn a part of the job. If the *Post* was a source of island news, its editor was a community friend, and he couldn't imagine what life would be without a daily call for help or advice.

One of the paper's most faithful readers was the editor of a Boston daily who followed the work of Joe Hurley, who, in simple emotional prose, wrote of the loneliness and isolation of those living in the long wintry solitude. Joe wrote of the drinking, the violence, the passions of ordinary men and women. But of the passion ruling his own heart, of that passion, Joe Hurley was silent.

⸙

FINN AND JOE HURLEY, COUSINS, BOYHOOD FRIENDS, and close as brothers and that is how they regarded each other. Finn had a sunny disposition, as though an inner light were warming him, while Joe, a more interior man, was rugged, shy, and less given to talk, yet the two men shared a warmth of spirit and a goodness of heart that spoke to every action of their lives.

As boys, they rolled cigarettes and puffed away. They fished, set lobster traps, hunted for rabbits, and rode the deserted beaches on horses borrowed from a neighboring farmer. They laughed at everything and thought the world would end if they didn't talk a half dozen times a day.

They pretended they were Knights of the Round Table. Finn was King Arthur, and Joe was Sir Lancelot. They were polite and courteous, always ready to assist. Yet something was missing from their world of good deeds, and until they found her, they didn't realize they had been in search of a damsel in distress. And the whole time she had been right under their noses, the poor beautiful girl who sang and danced on street corners. My mother, Claire, was a gallant young knight's dream come true.

If the two young men had been insensitive to her plight, they would atone for it the rest of their lives. They scraped up money to buy her a new warm coat, and one by one replaced the shabby dumptique discards with clothes bought on sale at the Pequod Emporium.

The *Post* was always struggling for advertisers, so Finn suggested to his father he hire Claire to sell space. She turned out to be a natural-born saleswoman. Claire pleased, delighted, cheerfully refused to take no for an answer, and against all better judgment, the most frugal old Yankee broke down and placed an ad.

One old skinflint warned her, "You be careful, girl. You got too much charm for your own good."

Claire took his money and laughed.

"If I'm going to make a place for myself in this tough old world, I need all the charm I can muster."

Claire couldn't believe the boys' kindness or her newfound good luck. A matter of months and she had gone from begging in the streets and foraging at the dump to being an honest-to-goodness salaried employee on a newspaper.

On the hottest of days she strutted around in her new winter coat.

"So what if it's hot, or if my coat gets old and worn, it's my good-luck coat, and I'll never let it go."

Finn looked at her with worshipful eyes. She said, "You bring me luck, Finn. You and Joe are my two dearest friends, and I pray you'll never tire of my hanging around."

Tire of Claire! Finn looked into those deep yellow eyes and it felt like the heat of the sun. He was giddy at the sight of her, dizzy when she smiled; her cocky strut made him tingle with delight. Imagine! This bewitching creature asking him never to tire of her. Even if he tried he wouldn't know how, for Claire had put a lock on his heart and thrown away the key.

Those early years, they were the inseparable three. The boys shared Claire on a Saturday night, they cried at the movies and giggled over sodas. They swam in the wildest surf, fished off the old fisherman's bridge, skated on frozen ponds, and raced horses along the shore. Who could swim the fastest, stay underwater the longest, catch the biggest fish?

Who but Claire, who always won.

One day, she confronted them.

"I know you're humoring me," she said coolly.

"How do we humor you?"

"You let me win."

Joe laughed, but Finn, melting under her scorn, said, "No, we don't, Claire. We just accept you as the bravest, prettiest, most fearless girl we know."

"Poor Finn. You don't even know you're doing it."

"I want you to win," he said.

"There! You admit it! You're humoring me!"

"All right, I'll win. I promise. Next time I'll win."

"You're hopeless. A lost cause," she said, laughing.

And Finn, happy to be back in Claire's good graces, said, "I won't disappoint you. I'll win if it kills me."

Finn was deeply in love. It was in his eyes, the way he looked when Claire walked into a room or laughed at him or smiled. His eyes betrayed him, as did the way he blushed or went pale when she was nearby.

And Claire, aware of her power and delighting in it, ignored Finn's confusion. But Joe knew what was happening, and kept silent. Silence was his best protection. He knew Finn would suffer if he, in any way, responded, so he squashed all feeling, and was cool and detached. But no matter how he disguised what he felt, Joe knew he was vulnerable. Claire had laid siege to his heart too; he couldn't, he wouldn't, in any way respond.

Claire asked Joe, "Why is it if I dress like a girl, I get on your nerves, but when I dress like a boy, we go from being two knights and a damsel in distress to the Three Musketeers?"

"I don't care what you wear as long as you realize

Finn and I are two different people. If he treats you like a queen whose every word is his command, that's his business, but don't expect it from me."

"Why, Joe! You're protecting yourself."

"Protecting myself! From what?"

"From me, of course. Anyhow, it's not important. What's important is friendship, the three of us, all our lives."

Joe loved to fish by moonlight or in the early dawn, and sometimes Claire would join him. She cast her line and hummed the song she once sang in the streets.

Joe loved the sound of her voice, the sweet husky timbre, but he was silent, and Claire sang her song and mused.

"Isn't it strange how I'm drawn to the sea, as if we're connected, and that's the irony, for it was the sea that took my father."

Joe glanced at her face, so sweet and so grave, and a tremor passed through him, it passed between them, and Claire knew that Joe loved her, he had to love her, their souls had touched, and in the silence she was happy; this intensity, this strange and utter happiness, was just too much to bear.

Finn had never felt it before, and tried to ignore the jealousy tearing at his heart. He would gamble on Claire's coming to love him by becoming indispensable, a rock, a loving friend, the father figure she would turn to in sadness or triumph. He went as far as to counsel her in matters of love. When Claire worried Joe might be attracted to someone else, Finn swallowed the hurt and said, "Joe's a one-woman man. He doesn't do the chasing. It's the girls who chase after Joe."

"Well, he won't get very far from me."

And seeing the look of distress on Finn's face, she added, "Nor will you, dearest Finn, for I need you more than ever before."

And in a rare moment of physical affection, Claire threw her arms around his neck, and Finn saw it as a sign of hope.

She doesn't love me yet, he thought, but Claire needs love, and I need Claire, and one day she'll understand what I offer, and that no one—no one—will ever love her as deeply as me.

❧

WHEN FINN AND JOE HAD ANOINTED CLAIRE AS THEIR damsel in distress, everything had been equal and shared, but they were older now. Finn giving himself over to the paper, and Joe writing for himself as well as reporting. They had matured into responsible men, while my mother's need for love and admiration seemed like an unquenchable thirst. If Claire passed herself off as a care-free young sport, she loved like an ill-fated heroine of a Puccini opera.

Claire knew Finn loved her, was sure Joe loved her too, but what my mother craved was constant unconditional love. Love, for my mother, had become a dangerous drug. Everyone must love her: the owner of the drugstore, the grocery clerk, bus drivers, waiters, and policemen; everyone must fall under her spell. Yet, when Claire spoke to a man, she made him feel like a god, so men didn't regard her as sluttish or crude, but as if she were a visiting movie star.

When Joe criticized her for her indiscriminate flirting, she wanted to say, "If you'd admit I'm your true love, I would never flirt again." Instead, she looked him in the eye and said, "I could apologize, call it a character flaw, but since I hurt no one . . . at least, no one but myself . . ."

She reached over to kiss him, but Joe pulled away.

Years later, he told me, "I longed to take her in my arms, tell her I loved her and was crazy with desire, but I couldn't hurt Finn, so I ignored my pounding heart and pretended to be amused."

THEY DID NOT SPEAK OF IT, BUT SOMETHING WAS happening, something unusual, something unexpected.

It had started much earlier, the first secret between them, both Finn and Joe guarding the fact they were in love with the same woman, who, under their eyes, had blossomed from a damsel in distress into a disturbing beauty. Both men were silent, unwilling to hurt or betray the other, yet Joe knew the first move was up to him; he would have to leave the island, stay away until it was safe to come home.

Except he wasn't ready, not yet, not emotionally. Still, something had to be done. He hadn't decided on a plan of action, but he knew Claire was mistress of her knights, she had laid siege, claimed them as her property, and it was getting out of control. He also knew Claire's independence was critical. It would free the three of them from what was becoming a crippling dependence. No way to disguise it, something had to be done.

I don't know how Joe came up with the idea of photography except no one had replaced Claire's father as town photographer, and Joe was sure a profession would free Claire from a financial and emotional dependence on Finn and himself.

There were problems, of course, and the first was equipment. Claire had her father's heavy old Graflex, but she needed a lightweight, flexible camera, a Leica or Rolleiflex. The other more serious question was one of craft. Who would teach her? Where would she learn?

Years earlier, Joe had interviewed Eugene Jones, a venerable old photographer who lived in a small house on a rise in the woods and ventured into town only to buy provisions or gas for his car. Joe told Finn he would speak to Jones about taking Claire on as a student.

Finn said, "That's inspired!" and the friends approached Claire.

"Eugene Jones was a legend in his lifetime," Joe told her, "but he was temperamental, a prima donna who insisted on creative control over his pictures appearing in the mass-market magazines. He was quarrelsome, abrasive, and had a fallout with an important picture editor who represented the policies of the owner.

"'If we give in to your demands, which are in conflict with ours,' said the editor, 'we'll be forced to give in to everyone's.'

"Jones was furious. He gave an interview to a *Times* reporter in which he said, 'I must have freedom to work. They're trying to suppress me, and I won't submit to censorship.' It caused a furor, and after that time there was an unspoken gray list against Jones, so he retreated to Pequod, where he lives like a hermit."

"Poor old fellow. Must be very angry," said Claire.

"I suspect he is."

"Then why would he agree to sell me a camera, much less teach me?"

"I suppose it's a gamble," said Joe. "But since you can charm a snake to rise up, maybe you can charm the old recluse into swapping a Leica for your father's old Graflex."

"My father's Graflex . . . It's all I've got left." Her voice was like ice.

"I'm sorry, Claire, I'm being insensitive and stupid, but Jones is a lonely old fellow and might be glad to help a beautiful . . . young . . ."

". . . damsel in distress," she said. "Okay, I accept your apology."

"Then I'll give him a call."

"Thank you very much, but I'm quite capable of calling Mr. Jones without any assistance."

EUGENE JONES HAD BEEN SLEEPING POORLY OF LATE, and was prone to sudden attacks of nausea. This afternoon, sprawled on a wicker lounge and warming himself in a late wan sun, he was listening to music as Claire's old Ford pulled into the driveway.

She slammed the car door shut, pulled a cap off her head, and a mass of reddish gold hair fell onto her shoulders. Yes, it was the same girl but grown into a graceful beauty. Eugene watched as Claire approached. The sound of music was coming from the house.

"Brahms," said Eugene. "I'm partial to Brahms."

Claire cocked her head and listened.

"It's sad," she said. "So beautifully sad."

"It pleases but doesn't surprise me you've a taste for Brahms. I once suspected you'd be a romantic."

"Then we've met before?"

Eugene pulled himself up from the chair and walked toward the house. He turned at the door and said, "Well, Claire, are you coming?"

"I'm right behind you."

They entered a sparsely furnished room with a couch, a table and four wooden chairs, an easy chair for reading, and a bed. One wall was lined with filing cabinets. It was a room unused to visitors, and Claire felt she was violating Eugene's privacy, yet his warm inviting welcome made her feel as if he had been waiting for her to come.

"Mr. Jones," she repeated. "Do you know me?"

Eugene Jones went to a filing cabinet. He pulled out a drawer, fingered a group of manila folders, pulled one out, took it to the table, and opened it.

"Come close, Claire. Look at my pictures, and I think you'll understand."

Claire saw glossy prints of a young girl, singing, dancing, passing a hat, and smiling, always smiling, on each picture the girl wore a smile.

"Well, what do you think?"

"I think I'm in shock."

"No, no. What do you think of the pictures?"

"They're sad, aren't they? Yet, in some strange and fateful way, I feel as if they've led me here."

"Not fate, Claire, luck. I've had my camera on you a

good long time, and I was curious. I made inquiries. Discovered your father was a photographer with a shop on Main Street. Heard he died in some freak explosion at sea and your mother, poor soul, became the town drunk. So when I got your call, I said, Eugene, this young woman needs your help. So tell me, Claire, tell the old photographer what he can do."

Claire hesitated.

"Don't be shy, girl, speak up."

"I want to be a photographer, Mr. Jones, but I need a camera and, more important, I need someone to teach me."

"Don't you have a camera?"

"My father's old Graflex."

"Ever use it?"

"No."

"Ever take a picture?"

"Snapshots."

"I'm sure you've heard of Eugene Jones's reputation."

"Yes, sir. I have."

"And what have you heard?"

"That you're temperamental, world famous, I mean, like a legend, and, oh yes, a genius."

"And why would a temperamental old crotchety genius take the time to teach photography to a girl who's never taken a picture?"

"I don't think he would."

Eugene laughed. "Well, at least you're honest, but you haven't answered my question."

"The answer's in that folder. The pictures of the happy smiling beggar. That's your answer. I want to learn photography so I'll never have to beg again."

"And what about boys? I would think they're buzzing around you like bears around a honey pot."

"Not the one I love."

"I think I understand. Some years ago, a handsome young man came to interview me for the *Post*."

"His name's Joe Hurley."

"And this Joe Hurley is the one you're in love with?"

"Yes."

"And Joe Hurley suggested you call me?"

"Yes."

"And you want to make him proud of you, show Joe Hurley you're a gifted photographer, maybe give love a little push."

"Maybe give it a great big push."

"Not a very good reason for me to take you under my wing, but as you share my feeling for Brahms, I'm going to take a chance on giving this love story a happy ending. I've got an old Leica I don't use. It's a genius of a camera, but it's not going to take the pictures. That is up to you . . . for God's sake, Claire, no tears. You embarrass me, girl."

"I'm sorry . . . it's that . . . you're so kind . . ."

"Me! Eugene Jones, kind! I thought you knew the great man's reputation. Had to have his way; mocked this and mocked that; put up barbed wire between the world and myself. Well, it's too late to turn back the clock and even if I could, I'm not sure I could have done it any other way. In any case, I'm taking you on as my student, and if you've got the gift, by the time we're finished, you'll be a damned good photographer. And, dear girl, you'll find there's more to life than the curse of an aching heart."

"Is that what I feel?"

"So claim the poets. Well, let's begin."

Eugene showed Claire how to load the camera, then he took her outside and raised his hand against the sun.

"Tell me, Claire, what do you see?"

"A silhouette of your hand."

He turned it in the opposite direction, and it was sunlit.

"Now what do you see?"

"I see every line in your hand."

"And that is our first lesson: to understand light is like the sun. As basic as that, it is light that sculpts the planes of a face. Light and shadow are your tools in capturing the essence of personality, and that is what a good portrait does, it reveals who a man or woman is.

"That's it for today." Eugene said. "Now listen closely, Claire. Pequod is a microversion of the world. I want you to take your Leica, go into Pequod, and shoot a couple rolls of film. Drop them in my mailbox. I'll develop the negatives, and next week we'll print."

"Will I ever be able to thank you? I mean really thank you, Mr. Jones?"

"You'll become the photographer I want you to be. That will be my reward."

Claire walked the path to her car. She turned, blew Eugene a kiss, smiled, and drove away.

⚯

THE FOLLOWING WEEK, CLAIRE ARRIVED DRESSED AS a boy.

"One day, I'll photograph you in yellow and catch the gold in those luminous eyes," said Eugene, "but now, let's get started. You've got a lot to learn."

Claire followed him into a room that served as a darkroom.

"I've developed your negatives and I'm going to take you through a simple process of printing. Remember, I said light and shadow complement each other, that light and shadow reveal the passion of a soul."

"I remember."

"Let's see how you've used them."

Eugene showed Claire how to dilute the developing solution for a soft dreamy print and how to intensify it for a hard granite effect. Then, using a pair of wooden tongs, he lifted the wet prints from the solution and hung them from wires strung across the room.

"Primitive, but it serves me," he said.

He developed pictures of clouds and trees, dappled beaches, scurrying beach birds, and empty sunlit streets.

"They're pretty," said Claire. "And I'm pleased."

"Yes, they're pretty. Postcard pretty."

"You don't like them."

"You're playing it safe, my girl."

"Me? Play it safe!"

"Which is not a very good reason for me to spend my time and energy teaching you what I know."

"What do you want, Eugene? Tell me."

"I want you to understand a camera is only a machine. It's your eye, Claire, your inner eye that takes the picture. Once you're in the darkroom, you can tinker and crop, move in to create illusion or reality, but it must be on the film. All I see are pretty pictures."

"And this inner eye. How do I find it? How do I use it?"

"It's your brain. It's your heart. It's your emotional core. I'm going to teach you how to use it, how to trust it, and you will begin to take pictures with a real emotional impact."

"And you believe I can do it?"

"I believe you can, I'm sure of it. But now it's time we put away our toys and listen to—"

"Brahms."

"To a ravishing Brahms quartet."

When Claire left Eugene that afternoon, her brain was on fire. She no longer felt like a smiling wind-up doll who charmed her way into the hearts of strangers. She felt a new confidence, the enthusiasm of a young woman about to embark on a great adventure, and if the adventure was to be had on a small island off the coast of Massachusetts, it seemed to Claire like the whole wide world.

❦

Don't just look! Look hard!" Eugene said, and Claire began to look hard. In a storm, she looked at ships straining against their moorings—would she ever escape her father's death? She looked into the eyes of poverty, the ravaged face of an old Indian, a blind man and his wife, a banged-up car, a toadstool growing by her father's grave, aimless kids with nothing to do and nowhere to go, the torn fluttering poster of an old movie. She looked at her tree in the meadow by the cliffs; all the loneliness she had run from she confronted in the lens of her camera.

Claire fell upon the craft of it with a kind of passion, as if photography would save her from her obsession with Joe. She didn't know how and she didn't care, she only knew she could lose herself in her work, that it brought relief instead of longing.

No longer an abandoned girl begging on street corners, she was becoming an aggressive young photographer. Admire a picture, you received it as a gift.

Claire's rough-hewn talent, charm, and generosity began to pay off.

The owner of a Main Street café offered to hang her pictures and split the money from sales. Claire made three hundred and twenty dollars. She took Eugene, Finn, and Joe out to celebrate.

"To Claire," the men toasted, and raised their glasses. She raised her glass and clinked it. "To making loads of money," she said, "and never ever smiling for a dollar again."

Claire went to the Fogg and Gardner museums in Boston and studied the great portraits. When she returned to the island, she said to Joe, "Of course I'll take pictures of the summer women, but they really don't interest me. What does interest me is a man's brain, the way he thinks."

"You fake," said Joe. "The only thing that interests you is having every man you meet fall wildly in love."

"Why, Joe. I do believe you're jealous."

"Me? Jealous!"

"Poor Joe. I'm afraid it's out of your control."

Claire stood in the sunlight, teasing and taunting, a lock of reddish hair falling on her face, and Joe thought her maddeningly lovely, but whatever he felt, he reined himself in.

"You're a terrible flirt, Claire. Be careful. Jealousy is a dangerous weapon, and someone can get hurt."

"Me? Hurt anyone?"

"Just be careful."

"I'll be careful. I promise, no one will ever be hurt."

⟨꧁⟩

Time and again, Joe tried to leave the island and the girl he loved, a girl Finn loved as well, and silent about his conflict, Joe avoided Claire, became brusque and detached, but he couldn't turn it off, this burn of desire, or the crippling passivity that kept him from taking action.

And Claire, sensing Joe's confusion, said, "I know you want to leave, but Pequod's in your blood, and though you won't admit it, I am too. I'm in your head, Joe, in your heart, and that's the reason you don't go."

Jealousy! Finn tried to fight it, but like an insidious poison it festered inside him, destroyed any peace of mind. There had to be an answer, an escape from the torment and feeling of helplessness. Perhaps the wisest course would be to confront Joe with the truth, tell him of his suffering and ask for Joe's help. Maybe together, they would come up with a cure.

It was a raw, damp day. Finn and Joe walked on the beach. They wore heavy jackets and kept their hands in their pockets, spoke aimlessly at first, then, abruptly, Finn switched the subject to Claire.

"If a stranger asked me to describe her, I'd call her the island Venus. I'm not sure even Claire knows her own seductive power."

"I'm sure she knows."

"So it's normal we're both under her spell. You've never said you love her, but I know you do, you know I do, and we could go on indefinitely, the best of friends in love with the same woman. Except it's not working. The truth is, she's hit me like an earthquake, and it's gotten worse. I could console myself with another woman, but I don't want anyone but Claire . . . I wouldn't be capable."

"I know."

"I long for the old innocence, but it's gone, Joe, gone. I'm jealous, I'm disturbed, and I need help. You're the only one I can turn to."

"Give me time," Joe said softly. "I'll find a way out, I promise."

꧁꧂

THE WAY OUT CAME WITH THE MURDER OF MARTIN McRae, a wealthy Rhode Island visitor who impregnated a Pequod girl with a promise of love. When she discovered she was nothing more than an August fling, she bought a gun, went to Providence, and shot her handsome lover outside his house.

In tough-minded yet sentimental prose, Joe covered the story of lust and betrayal. It was read by his admiring Boston editor, who time and again had offered Joe a job. This time, it was the way out, a way of being close to the island yet distant enough, and Joe accepted at once.

Joe told Claire he had accepted a job on a Boston newspaper, and with a good brave face she said, "I knew one day you'd leave, but I know you'll be back; you have to come back, Joe, and I'll be waiting."

"Maybe you're right and I am just a prodigal son, but I'm taking the job, Claire, and no one, no one, is changing my mind."

Finn and Claire stood on the dock, waving and watching as the ferry pulled away, and Claire wiped the tears from her eyes. Finn put an arm around her shoulder.

"I know you want to help, Finn, but all I want is to be left alone."

She pulled out of his grasp, walked to her car, and without looking back, drove away.

JOE MOVED TO BOSTON, AND A GIRL NAMED GIGI with long legs and a small waist chose him for her lover. Joe didn't resist. Gigi was a way of being free of Claire, except it didn't work. He made love to Gigi, thought of Claire, and knew, even if he wanted it, he wasn't free. Claire's power was too strong. He plunged into work, into sex, thought about Claire, felt guilty toward Finn, and accepted the fact they were bound together, the three of them, one for all and all for one; whatever was fated, affected them all.

⟨◌⟩

IT WAS SAVAGE THAT WINTER, THE WORST ONE IN YEARS; pounding winds and icy drifts made travel dangerous, if not impossible, but every week Claire went to see Eugene. He was pale and thin and she filled his refrigerator. The following week she would return with fresh provisions but find the last week's food barely touched.

"You promised me, Eugene, said you'd take care of yourself."

"Don't scold."

"I'm not scolding. I'm caring."

"Food's not the problem. Problem's my head. I'm a forgotten man, Claire, a piece of debris. I'm wrenched loose from the human race and gone to rot."

"No, Eugene, you're an artist. A brilliant photographer."

"I squandered my gift, and I can only blame myself. Things had to be my way, and my way was control. I'm inflexible, Claire. I used to call it artistic integrity, and the consequence is I'm a lonely old recluse, dependent on the generosity of a beautiful young woman who, I am delighted to say, shows every promise of becoming a fine photographer."

"One who wants to make money."

"Is that what you really want?"

"You know what I want."

It was one of the rare times Eugene laughed.

"I'm not a sentimental fellow, but if I had a daughter, I'd want her to be exactly like you. I hope you realize you've given your old friend some pretty happy hours."

"And look at all you've given me."

"Listen, Claire, and don't interrupt. My house is small, my files disorderly, but one day my photographs will be collector's items. Remember that! And now, I want to photograph a girl who loves Brahms, the essence of a romantic. And I'm going to show you how I work."

But Eugene sat down instead. He closed his eyes and leaned against the table.

"What is it, Eugene? Are you okay?"

"Damned dizzy spell. It'll pass in a minute."

"I'll call a doctor."

"For God's sake, don't clutter my life with doctors."

"Then promise, promise me you'll go for a checkup."

"Best medicine I know is taking your picture."

Eugene sat very still. When he stood, he walked to the cabinet, took out a camera, and indicated Claire was to sit in a chair by a window.

He was quiet and intent and Claire smiled and thought about Joe. She would give him Eugene's portrait, and Joe would keep it beside his bed. He would look at it on waking, and in the evening before falling asleep. *Oh, Joe . . . Joe . . . how can I bear to be without you?*

"Where's that smile? Where did it go? All I see are sad, sad eyes."

Eugene clicked the camera, and Claire said, "It's no use. I'm sorry. . . ."

"What happened? Tell old Eugene why you're suddenly sad."

"Not sad. Empty. The same old emptiness, and only free of it when Joe smiles or touches me. He called this morning. Said he thought he'd be able to write about people who interested him, but it's turned out to be a desk job with long confining hours, so he's told his boss he'll stay on if the paper lets him write what they promised, and they've agreed to a trial series of articles, which means he's not coming home, Eugene, and I don't know what to do."

"I know men, Claire, and I promise you Joe won't be able to stay away. . . ."

Eugene, suddenly tired, shut his eyes and clung to the chair.

"I'll come tomorrow," said Claire.

"Yes, tomorrow. Come back tomorrow, and we'll shoot our portrait then."

"I'll stay until you're feeling stronger."

"No, Claire, I want to rest."

She leaned over, kissed his cheek, and said, "In case you didn't know, I love my temperamental old genius."

"That's my best medicine, Claire, exactly what I need. You come tomorrow and I'll take some unforgettable pictures. And mark my words, one day they'll be extremely valuable."

⟨❧⟩

THAT NIGHT IT STORMED. THE ROADS WERE BURIED under heavy drifts. The following morning Claire called Eugene, said the roads were impassable and she couldn't get through, but she would be with him the following day.

"Just as well," he said. "I've had a sleepless night, and I'm very tired."

Was it simply old age or something more serious? Claire was right, he should see a doctor, and would, as soon as the snow melted. The doctor would find a reason for the dizzy spells, for the pain in his side he drugged with an old medication.

Why had he never mentioned it to Claire, he wondered, but he knew the answer, some old macho pride. Eugene Jones was invincible. Nothing could hurt Eugene Jones. Eugene Jones was too goddamn proud. All his life he had been an onlooker, had witnessed feeling but not experienced it, pounced on emotion through the lens of

38

a camera. Yes, it was finally time to admit he was only human, no different from anyone else. That was what Claire had taught him, it was all right to be vulnerable, not a man outside the human race but a part of it, a witness, yes, *and* a participant.

Am I in love? Has my lovely Claire broken through this crusty old shell and melted my heart? Suppose I'd met her when I was younger. I might be a different man today.

It was good to lie there with his eyes closed and think of her smile, the smile of a child, and think of her soft-as-velvet eyes and how wonderfully young they made him feel. Eugene thought about the pictures he would take, how he would focus on the eyes, the intensity of her eyes looking into yours, her angelic smile . . .

And suddenly, it was gone, Claire's image was gone, and Eugene was lost to encompassing darkness.

When he opened his eyes, it was night. He must have fallen asleep. He did not want to risk another dizzy spell so he lay on the couch and looked out the window and watched the moon rise and begin its ascent. The wind had died down. There were stars in the sky, and Eugene thought about Claire and how he would turn her into the photographer he knew she had it in her to become.

After a while he felt stronger. Eugene got up, made a pot of tea, and listened to a record of the Budapest playing a Brahms quartet. He loved the passion of their playing, and he listened to the Brahms, thought about Claire, thought about his camera, his negatives, and the prints of his work. These were his legacy, his gift to the plucky young woman who had brought him such happiness, and then it hit again, another sudden attack.

I'll be quiet and it will pass, he said to himself, but it lingered on. Again he vowed to see a doctor, but before anything else, there was something he must do, must attend to immediately. Eugene sat at the table and, by sheer force of will, put pencil to paper and began to write.

Dearest Claire,

These cameras are my children. Now they are yours. I want you to have them. They are sensitive and needy and, like all children, require care and attention. Care for them, Claire, and they will take care of you. And remember Eugene's wise words, "Look hard, but let your heart take the picture."

The Brahms quartet was over, and Eugene replayed it from the beginning. He lay on the couch and looked out the window. The moon was cold and silvery and he watched it sink into the sea. Soon the sun would rise. The roads would be cleared, and Claire would come and sit for a portrait. He would teach her everything he knew, secrets he had never before given away. She would have his camera, his negatives, all of his prints. It was his way of saying thank you.

A faraway clock struck the hour, church bells chimed: nine times, ten, eleven times, twelve.

There was a hurried sound of footsteps, a knock on the door, the doorknob twisting, and Claire rushed to Eugene's side. She kneeled beside his body and cried; tears of love for the darling old photographer who had been like a father, the father she yearned for, the father she had, at long last, found. Claire cried. She cried and cried, unable to stop.

∞

Joe returned for the funeral. Half a dozen people came to the old island church to pay their respects. Claire gave the eulogy.

"Eugene Jones lived like a recluse but his work affected us all. Week after week, we saw it in the big picture magazines, and when he no longer photographed and retired to Pequod, he saw his influence in the work of younger men. Eugene was an artist. He didn't play by the rules because rules are for good photographers, and Eugene Jones was a great one. If he seems a forgotten man today, one day the world will remember his work."

Afterward, Claire said, "I feel as if my heart is breaking."

"Eugene believed in you," said Joe. "You'll become the photographer he wanted you to be."

"Will I? I wonder." And changing the subject, she said, "How soon will you be leaving?"

"This afternoon. After I write Eugene's obituary."

"That's too soon."

"Only for a few days. I'll organize my things in Boston, come back and spend a week with you and Finn."

"And after that, you'll go. You'll really leave—"

"Claire will be fine," Finn interrupted. "I'll make sure she works and keeps busy. I can use you at the paper, Claire. There's plenty to do."

Late that afternoon, Joe gave Finn the obituary.

"I know this is a difficult time," said Finn.

"Yes, leaving is difficult. Pequod's about the most simple basic instincts and if it's old-fashioned and provincial, the sea, the sky and trees have a hold on my soul. I'm always drawn back, Finn, never free of its power."

But Finn knew Joe was really saying Claire's hold over him was as strong as before. Finn knew the situation would resolve itself, that it was a matter of time, of patience, a matter of fate. All Joe was doing was giving fate a little shove.

FINN AND CLAIRE WERE HAVING COFFEE IN A CAFÉ on Main Street. Joe was due on the two o'clock ferry.

"Pick me up at the office, and we'll meet him together," said Finn.

"No, Finn, not today. I want to meet him alone."

"What's the matter, Claire? Tell me what's wrong."

"What's wrong is you won't take me seriously."

"On the contrary. I take you very seriously."

"Then why don't you understand?"

"I do understand."

"Do you, Finn? Understand that from the very first moment, when I saw Joe on a sandy stretch at the foot of the cliffs, I fell in love. I smiled and he smiled back. Then he started to climb. When he reached the top he waved and disappeared. I started to tremble. I'm still trembling, Finn. I'm no good for you. I wouldn't make you happy."

"And I'm no good without you. Joe's a good, brave man and I know you love him, but he's like a bird that's ready for flight. Whoever tries to clip his wings will find herself with a wreck."

"You still don't understand."

"I understand his life seems glamorous while mine seems monotonous. And I could say I'll sell the paper, get a job on the mainland, and pretend to be happy, but it would be a lie. I don't want to live my life as a lie, so I'm being honest. I love you, Claire. I'll give you a home, a family, safety. We'll run the paper together. It'll be our paper, yours and mine. You'll take pictures, have children, and you'll be happy. I'll make you happy. Joe will bring you heartache."

"You don't listen, Finn. You don't hear me."

"I do hear you."

"What did I say?"

43

"That you aren't good for me and wouldn't make me happy."

"Then you understand."

"I understand what you want, what you think you want: kisses like fireworks, a cosmic collision. And for a while you'll have it. But fireworks fizzle, they die, and I'm afraid you'll be burned."

"If that's the price, I'll pay it."

And Claire's voice softened, as if the years of friendship were too important to jeopardize.

"I'm going to meet Joe alone and going to tell him how I feel."

She walked to the door and, without looking back, shut it behind her.

And there was Joe, crossing the gangplank and walking toward her, and Claire, bursting with excitement, felt she could fly straight into the sun, and if she burned her wings, who cared? The fall was worth the flight. Then Joe was beside her and the warmth of his smile felt like the heat of the sun.

Claire had heard about a girl in Boston, but she had no proof, only rumor and hearsay alerting her to a possible threat, so she raised her mouth for a kiss, but it wasn't only a kiss, she was blocking out the girl in Boston and every other girl. No, it wasn't a kiss, it was the heat of the sun, binding him, blinding him, to anyone but her.

"Can't you be the least bit patient?" he said and pulled away.

"I'm afraid not."

Joe laughed and mussed her hair.

"You're a bad girl to put me through all this."

"All this what?"

"You know damned well what."

She smiled and said, "I've got something to tell you. Let's drive out to my tree."

Joe pulled his valise from the gurney, and they got into her car. The sky was darkening. It started to rain. Claire turned on the windshield wipers. The rain stopped. She turned them off and parked the car. They walked to the tree, listened to the breaking waves and the cries of gulls.

"I miss all this," said Joe. "And I miss going fishing."

"I miss that too. One day we'll fish for salmon in the Columbia River."

"One day," he said.

"We'll go to the Pacific, far away from Pequod. We'll fish in Half Moon Bay and go down to Ensenada and fish off the beach. We'll sleep in funky hotels and when we come home, we'll fish off the bridge, like the old fishermen, and talk about the great fishing we've done."

"That's a sweet dream."

Claire put her arm around his neck. She watched him smile, that sweet defensive smile that was his way of distancing himself, of not telling her what he was feeling, but Claire knew what he was doing, and what did it matter? All the love she craved was in his eyes, in the way he moved when she touched him.

45

"Don't, Joe. Don't pull away."

And Joe, excited, hot, and fighting for control, knew that if he let himself go, he might never come back, and what about Finn? Finn was already suffering. He couldn't destroy him.

"I told Finn I love you. He knows, Joe, I don't have to pretend."

"Finn is like my brother. I won't hurt him."

"But you'll hurt me. You love me, Joe, you know you do, and you're willing to sacrifice me to some old game of boyhood loyalty. It's not fair, not fair to me, or you, or Finn."

"My staying on wouldn't solve anything. The best thing was for me to stay away, to write about the people I've always wanted to write about."

"It won't work, Joe. I won't marry Finn."

"And I won't marry you."

Claire pulled him close and the feel of her body, alive and intense, made him crazy. Neither spoke but love was there, in her kisses, like the swell of a wave, wave after wave of her, sucking him under, and Joe knew he must act. If he wavered, delayed, or stopped to reconsider . . . No, he couldn't hurt Finn. It was time to let Claire go.

WITH JOE GONE FROM THE ISLAND, CLAIRE SEEMED to collapse. She no longer rode the great white horse Finn rented from a local farmer, or swam the chilly waters of the sound, or fished or raced or strutted about. She had been in love with Joe for as long as she could remember, and with the steely discipline of an old sergeant had disguised what she felt, until now, and now it didn't matter. Joe was gone and nothing mattered.

Claire shut herself away in the house in the woods Eugene had left her. She kept the blinds half drawn, shut out the world, and played and replayed a fantasy of Joe, the way he looked and moved, the sound of his voice, again and again, until fantasy took her over and crowded out everything else.

Claire knew Joe loved her, he had to love her. If she was patient and persevered, one day he would falter or stumble, he would tire of the chase.

And as Claire replayed old scenes and dreamed of Joe, she began to make order and study Eugene's pictures.

"I've been all over the world," he'd once said. "I've seen everything, every sort of suffering and loneliness, happiness, despair, and it's all here, on our little island. Pequod is a microcosm of the world, Claire. You don't have to leave or go elsewhere for a subject. Your subject is here."

And suddenly, instinctively, she knew fate had led her to Eugene, and knew photography would save her.

Finn was not about to be chucked out of her life. He cared for Claire as you would a sick child, made sure she ate, nagged when she didn't, dragged her out to dinner or a movie. Yet all his love and concern didn't ease his jealousy. He tried to control it, joked, was his old amiable self, but it was there, playing havoc with his nerves, and he was at its mercy.

He wondered if Claire suspected. Their eyes would meet and he felt she did. But then she'd smile, or show a rare display of physical affection, and in those seconds, hope, like a mirage, seemed within his grasp.

This was Finn's secret, and if she knew, Claire was silent. She didn't laugh or mock him, and only occasionally said, "It embarrasses me, Finn, when you stare at me like that."

"Am I staring? I'm sorry."

"Why can't you accept how wrong I am for you?"

"No, Claire, you're right for me."

"Oh, Finn, don't you see how different we are? You were born to be steady, caring, and old and I was born to be young. That's what attracts you, makes you think you can save me, but you can't, you can't save me or change me. I'm the way I am, the way I was born, wrong for you in the same way you're wrong for me."

But Finn persevered.

"I may not have your fantasy of romance on the high

seas, but I love you, and if I was born steady and caring, born an old soul, my love for you is young, tender, and unconditional; it's the way I am, the way I was born."

◯◯◯

JOE WROTE REGULARLY, AT FIRST.

> *I've gone deep into rural America, and I'm trying to report what I see, the terrible poverty of what's called an underclass, incarcerated boys, hungry families. Oh, God, the hunger; I feel as if I'll never capture the suffering and harshness of these lives, but I'll keep trying, and eventually, I hope to make sense of it all.*
>
> *One thing I know is how much I miss you. You are the two people I love most in this world.*
>
> *Love,*
> *Joe*

Then his letters became infrequent. There was a long dry spell, and finally one arrived.

> *I've been sick. I thought it was the loneliness, but it's more than emotion. It's stomach pain so severe I'm close to collapse. Next big town I'm seeing a doctor . . .*
>
> *Love again,*
> *Joe*

Then Joe phoned from a hospital.

"They're doing tests," he said. "The intensity of the spasms seems to indicate kidney stones. They'll operate tomorrow, and hopefully, I'll be free of pain."

"You'll convalesce in Pequod," said Finn.

Claire pulled the phone from his hand. "Oh, Joe, come home. As fast as possible. Please, Joe, we'll take care of you here."

So Joe returned to the island and his recovery became Claire's sole concern. She nursed him, cooked for him, flirted with him, and was her old seductive self.

"Now you're stronger and you'll be leaving soon and I'll only be a memory, but no matter where you go, if you find another woman, pretend I don't exist, it won't work, Joe, we're fated."

"You're like a cat playing with a poor weak mouse. Aren't you ashamed?"

"Poor weak mouse who thinks he'll get away."

"I'm not fated and neither are you, Claire, but I'm glad you have such a good time talking about it."

"You love me."

"I don't love you."

"You do love me, possessiveness and all."

"Is love all you think about? The only thing you can talk about?"

"Don't try and distract me, because it won't work. Relax and accept I'm your fate, and you're mine."

She kissed him playfully and laughed.

And Joe knew, body and soul he knew, that one day the mouse would tire and submit to its fate.

⁘

Wᴛʜ Jᴏᴇ's ʀᴇᴄᴏᴠᴇʀʏ, Cʟᴀɪʀᴇ's ʟɪsᴛʟᴇssɴᴇss ᴅɪs-appeared. There was a light in her eye and a bounce to her step. Finn saw the change and knew he must act. He wasn't sure what to do or what change would bring, but the situation was intolerable. Something must be done and it was up to him. He was convinced his love for Claire was unconditional, convinced it was selfless, could survive, yes, surmount any obstacle. That's what Finn thought, and he spent nights grappling with his emotions, slipping from gloomy visions of loss and loneliness to ones of requited passion.

Then, one sleepless night, lying in the dark, clear and bright it came to him, the answer to his prayer. A simple matter of mathematics. His mistake had been in fantasy, seeing love as the coupling of two souls, Romeo and Juliet, Antony and Cleopatra, Finn Hurley and Claire, but the numbers were wrong. It had always been the three of them, one for all and all for one; why not simply, but legally, go on as before?

But for his plan to succeed he needed Joe's help. And why in God's name wouldn't Joe agree, for Joe loved Claire too? Oh, not with the same selfless passion—and

51

Finn stopped himself and smiled at the notion of passion being selfless, but reasoned that if a man loves hard enough, and is determined enough, passion can be reined in and tamed. The problem was how: how to make it work?

The first step would be to discuss it with Joe in a private and neutral place over dinner and drinks. Yes, he would need a couple of martinis to bolster his courage. . . .

Then he thought of Claire's fury when she discovered he had talked to Joe without including her, as if Joe and he were in collusion.

He could hear Claire's cool disdainful voice: "You call me your equal but treat me like a child."

And he heard himself, on the defensive: "I thought it was a solution, an end to frustration and heartache, but I needed Joe's consent."

No, he must include Claire or she would regard it as a betrayal of trust and never forgive him.

And so, days later, the two knights and their damsel in distress sat in a restaurant, talking and reminiscing, until Joe, realizing the intake of gin was only a prelude to something more serious, said, "Tell us, Finn, before we're stinking drunk, what's the reason we're here."

Finn swallowed his drink and ordered another.

"I've brought us together to discuss what's on our minds, what we've avoided facing, what's become a burden for us all. . . ."

He faltered, looked at Claire, and found the courage to go on.

"I don't know if Claire's told you, but I've asked her to marry me. I knew she'd say no, that she'll continue to say no, and I know she's stubborn as a mule, and will wait as long as she has to, to get what she wants. Well, Claire wants you and I want Claire, and that's why we're here, to be honest with each other, to try and work out a course of action. So, Joe, be honest, are you going to marry Claire?"

"No, Claire. I'm not going to marry you."

Before she reacted, Finn said, "Which leaves us with an ongoing and unresolved dilemma. Here we are, the best of old friends, in love with the same woman. The three of us are frustrated and unhappy. That's the problem. What's the answer? Is there a solution? Well, I think there is. No, I'm not crazy, not some lunatic in love. Because we're so close and such good friends, I'm sure my plan will work."

Finn paused and looked into Claire's eyes.

"I know Joe would marry you if he didn't feel such loyalty to me. And I know you don't, well, feel the same emotional intensity for me that you do for Joe, but I offer the safety of home and family. Not a madman in love, Claire, but a realist who's been in love with you from the first moment he saw you. I'm still in love, and willing to have you on any terms."

"What are you talking about?"

"I'm saying I want to share you!"

"Share me!"

"That's right. I want to share you with Joe."

"You call yourself a realist," Joe said, "and perhaps on the mainland, where attitudes are open and more sophisticated, your plan might work, but we live on an island, in a small provincial community, and I doubt if we stand a chance."

"Pequod is small and narrow-minded but who cares? And if you won't marry me, Joe—"

But Finn interrupted. "What's really bothering Joe is he thinks I'm getting the short end of the bargain. But I feel such strong love for our beautiful friend, I can turn the other way when I have to, and if it's got to be a triangular arrangement, that's how it's got to be. I'm prepared to gamble. If the three of us commit ourselves, it'll work. We'll make it work."

Everyone was silent. Then Finn said, "It's up to Claire."

Claire spoke in a soft voice. "It's true, none of the pieces fits, not in a conventional way, but it's like a puzzle, a human puzzle, and when the pieces don't fit, you rearrange them until they do."

"You're saying yes!" said Finn.

"You both know I'm greedy to be loved. I do want a home and child, and I also want romantic love, and the idea of being loved by my two adorable knights is irresistible. Anyhow, who loves who the most isn't important. What's important is we're together, and that, finally, someone's going to make a respectable woman out of me.

Oh, Joe, if you love me at all, say yes, yes for my sake, for all our sakes."

Joe laughed. "God forbid I should stand in the way of your becoming respectable."

"Then it's one for all and all for one," said Finn.

Everyone raised a glass.

"Here's to Claire in her quest for respectability." They clinked glasses and drained them.

"And now, the question of who will marry us."

"I will," said Joe. "The state of Massachusetts grants a one-day justice of the peace permit to anyone who wants to officiate at a marriage, which means I can marry you."

"Under my tree. That's what I want, it's where I want to be married."

"It's settled," said Finn, and placed his hand on the table, palm up. Joe put his hand on Finn's, and Claire took both in hers.

"To the three of us," she said, "to our peace, our pleasure, and our happiness."

Years later, Joe told me, "I tried to disguise what I felt. Claire knew I loved her but I was honor-bound to Finn, and the intensity of my desire had become a kind of torture. So when Finn came up with the wild idea of sharing Claire, I agreed. I know it's hard to believe, but we were so repressed, yet so full of love, it seemed a civilized solution."

. . .

And Claire, in her ongoing lifelong confession, said, "Marriage seemed like sanity, a way out of a hopeless situation. I thought Finn was a saint and believed him when he said he loved me with all the love in his heart, so despite my infatuation with Joe, and with a kind of blind faith, I said yes. Sharing seemed inspired. I would have them both, separately and yet together. I knew Finn loved me, and if Joe pretended indifference, I saw love in his eyes. Finn was right. It had been the three of us for so long, why shouldn't we go on? And I confess: it excited me. No longer a beggar on the streets, I was hungry for love, saw love as a magic charm . . . what I most craved.

"And it worked. Joe, Finn, and me, together and one. Yes, for a while, it worked."

I WANT TO BE MARRIED AT DAYBREAK," SAID CLAIRE. "I want the world all silvery and shining."

"A hell of an ungodly hour," said Finn.

"It's my wedding, Finn darling, and that's what I want, to be married at dawn under the branches of my dear old tree."

So Finn, Claire, Joe, and a witness from the *Post* stood beneath the gnarled old oak while a strangely somber Joe performed the ceremony. On one side, the waves pounded the cliffs, on the other, a path sloped toward the water and fell into the sea. My mother had never been so beautiful, my father so full of joy, for his one true love was, at long last, his wife.

The somber expression on Joe's face was not emotional restraint. He was in pain throughout the ceremony, and only afterward, on refusing a glass of champagne, did he admit to the old kidney disorder.

Claire said she would go home with him, Joe said he wanted to be alone and would join them for dinner, so she curbed her expectations and went home quietly with Finn. But that afternoon, Joe called, said he couldn't manage any food and was canceling for the wedding dinner.

For the next few days, Claire shuttled between the two houses and cooked for, nursed, and took care of Joe. When Finn finished with work, he went to visit Joe and left with Claire on his arm.

And under her ministrations, Joe was feeling stronger. But Claire sensed something was wrong and decided to confront him.

"What's happened? You've put a clamp on your emotions. Shut yourself up and shut me out. Why won't you be honest and tell me what's wrong?"

"Nothing's wrong."

"You're not being fair."

"I guess I'm not."

"Tell me, Joe. What's wrong?"

"What's wrong is when I look into Finn's eyes I see the hurt. I feel the pain in his heart. He doesn't say anything but I know that he suffers."

"What's wrong is you're punishing me for your guilty conscience."

"No, Claire, I'm not."

"Yes, Joe, you are."

"Whatever it is, there's a rift between Finn and me. I suppose I knew it would happen. I certainly knew the morning you were married. Whatever our agreement, I won't hurt him, Claire. Try to understand."

"Isn't it sad? We're so close to happiness and it frightens you."

"I'm not much good at being happy."

"Or being fair to me."

"Whoever said love was fair?"

"Finn did. This whole business was his idea. He said we'd be happy. It's the reason I agreed."

"He never said it was fair. He hatched up a plan so he could be with you, but he never called it fair."

"You're right, Joe. You're not much good at being happy, but you're wrong about Finn. He's not the one who's hurting. I am. Even worse is you don't see what you're doing."

"I'm sorry."

"I'm sorry too, sorry you're such a fool."

She moved against him, her breasts pressed to his chest, kissed and kissed him again, and when he moaned she knew she had him, he was defenseless, he was hers.

"You can't leave without me, Joe; please, darling, take me along."

But Joe was silent and all she felt was the hollow victory of his desire, but not a victory of love.

⁂

No matter how sanctioned and legal Claire's marriage, Pequod tongues were wagging. It was clear to the good island folk that something strange, something irregular, was going on between her and her two men. You couldn't miss the small-town back talk and gossip. But neither rumor nor exaggeration could stop them, and since the three caused no harm or damage, they continued on in their unconventional lifestyle and after a time came to be accepted as the Pequod bohemians. Finn's weekly newspaper was a compass of local life, Joe's column was devoured by its readers, and Claire was a lucky plucky girl who had pulled herself up from the gutter and had the good luck of marrying Finn.

And so, like old snow before a thaw, the rumors came to rest on the island's surface, melting away, barely leaving a trace.

CLAIRE WAS THE SORT OF BEAUTY WHO COULD have danced off to a big city and found a rich and powerful husband, but money and power were not the stuff of her dreams. Her dreams were of Joe, and she once told me, "He's put a match to my heart, and it's burst into flame."

In Claire's small unstable world, Finn's devotion and character, his vow of fidelity, of sharing her freely and unconditionally with her true love, were Claire's dream come true.

"It wasn't a barter or trade," she once told me. "It was equitable and fair. Marriage meant family, it meant safety, protection, and, most important, it was a way of being with Joe. I knew Joe loved me. I felt it in his glance, his touch, in the feel of his lips. If I was patient, he would come around and admit he loved me too. I could make it happen, of that I was sure."

If Joe had built a wall around his heart, Claire scaled the heights. He found himself thinking of her, dreaming of her, and denying how he felt. And he was pained by the growing divide between Finn and himself and knew he had no choice. He had to leave Pequod. Except he didn't. He postponed, procrastinated, was torn and conflicted, could barely look Finn in the eye.

Then, unexpectedly, Finn said, "It's time we talked. Let's take a walk on the beach."

It was an overcast day, with dark skies and wind-tossed waves. The men strolled along the water's edge.

"I'm stronger now," Joe said, in what sounded like an apology. "A few business details that will take a couple of days, and I'm ready to leave."

"Have you told Claire?"

"No, not yet."

"Be gentle with her, Joe. Try not to hurt her more than is necessary."

The men walked in silence and Finn said, "I know why you're leaving, Joe, I mean the real reason, and I hope you realize I know the rules of the game, and if ours is a game of too much love—"

"A surfeit of love."

"If that's what you want to call it, but it was my decision, and I had no choice. I must share Claire in order to have her. I know she loves you and that's the price I must pay. I also know you're worried I'll be hurt, but I've always been in love with Claire, and with all its complications, the limitations, she is finally my wife."

"Don't explain, Finn. I understand."

"It's important I say it. Without you, Claire suffers. Without her, I suffer. I look into those big sad eyes, see how she looks at me without seeing me, and it breaks my heart. God knows why I love her so, but I do, and if I seem like a lovesick adolescent, I'm also an optimist. I tell myself we'll adjust to the strange reality that's become our life, that it's a matter of time and things will work themselves out. I believe it, Joe."

"I hope to God you're right."

"I want you to know I know what I'm doing and I've got the strength to hang on. My love for Claire gives me that strength, it gives me faith in our future!"

Claire stood on the wharf, tears streaming down her cheeks. Joe wiped them away and kissed her on the forehead.

"I guess I'm putting you through hell."

"You're putting yourself through hell."

"Oh, Joe."

"You're so damned talented. That's what hurts me, that you fritter away a God-given gift."

"I've tried, Joe, shot roll after roll of film, but it feels mechanical, as if I'm on automatic. I've just lost interest."

"Suppose the milkman lost interest in delivering milk, or the pediatrician lost interest in babies, or the gardener in flowers, or Finn in the *Post*. I'm leaving Pequod to go back to work. What makes you so different from the rest of humanity? I want you to promise you'll put that over-romantic imagination of yours to work."

A quick kiss on the lips and he walked up the ramp to the ferry, waved, and disappeared.

Claire felt the old anxiety. Oh God, would it never end, this feeling of running on empty, of disguising her fear with charm and a strut? She had run from her fear, had risked any danger, but only with Joe was she free from its clutch.

"My sweet beloved," she whispered, "how can you leave me and what will I do?"

⁂

Finn EXPECTED THE DRAMATIC MOOD SWING THAT swept Claire up when Joe was away, and, determined to make his marriage a success, he became indispensable, soothed and sympathized, was like a loving father. But he was no match for Joe's claim on her heart and it seemed an almost futile struggle. So he tried a different approach.

"You see Joe as a primal force of nature," he said. "But Joe's only human, a man like other men, and you're a strong brave girl and you'll survive his absence."

"Bravery is a disguise and I'm sick of pretending. I wish things were different; wish we could live on the mainland where the odds weren't against us and we were like everyone else."

"I guess the odds are against us, against my making a go of a country newspaper, against the fisherman making a living off a brutal sea, against the farmer tilling the soil, knowing his crop can be destroyed by a winter storm. Yes, the odds are against us but Pequod's our home, our history. Our men fought in the Civil War—your great-great-grandfather photographed the destruction. They went to California and panned for gold, sailed the Arctic seas to make their fortune in whale oil, men like your father, who never returned. So honor his memory."

"Don't make me feel ashamed."

"Not ashamed, Claire, proud. Take your camera, go into the streets and down to the sea. Give Pequod a shape and a form. It's what Eugene Jones wanted, what Joe and I want. The odds are with you if you lose yourself in work. Trust me, Claire, work's the best medicine for a case of the blues."

He was very gentle, and Claire took his hand and pressed it to her lips.

"We'll have a baby," he said. "It's what we both want. If it's a boy we'll call him Joe."

Claire smiled, and he said, "And if it's a girl, she'll be our Joely."

"You're right, Finn, we'll have a Joe or a Joely, and we'll be happy, the way it used to be, the three of us, happy."

"The four of us," Finn corrected. "The three of us will soon be four."

CRXD

THE WINTER STORMS DIED DOWN, AND THE FURY OF the wind. Sunlight fell upon the cobbled streets. The sea was calm and blue. Claire looked at the maples, the towering elms, and the sassafras trees. She looked at the fishermen in their weather-beaten boats and thought about her father and how he perished at sea.

In the old Seaman's Cemetery, she knelt beside his grave and thought about her mother, who had watered it with whiskey and tears. The smell of lilac was in the air. She breathed it in and asked herself, "What is it I want to do?"

She wandered the meadows, the beaches, the old familiar paths in search of an answer, but an answer to what?

And then Claire was pregnant, and with her pregnancy she knew. It was so simple. She would return to the dump, to the discarded clothes and broken toys and unhinged furniture. The answer was in the lost world of her childhood. She would give it shape and form, the way Eugene wanted: she would give the dump a soul.

Joe returned to Pequod and built a darkroom for Claire while Finn converted a small unused room into the baby's quarters.

And Claire was happy; she had never been so happy. She spent mornings at the dumptique and came home to develop and print her film.

For as long as she remembered, she had drawn on her charm, once singing and dancing for dollars and dimes. Her smile had brought money and her smile had brought love, and suddenly, Claire found that when she lifted a camera to her eye, the burden of having to please was gone. No longer a street girl singing for change, she stepped aside from childhood wounds and, through the lens of a Leica, brought old emotion to a world of discard and junk.

And the baby was growing, larger and larger. Four months more, then three, then two and one, and Claire and Finn would be proud parents and Joe would be the godfather. If it seemed a flouting of morals in staid and provincial Pequod, Finn said the baby would bring order into their tangled messy lives.

❧

THE ARRANGEMENT WAS SIMPLE: JOE WAS TO LEAVE THE island for ten days, return for a week, and leave again. Before she was pregnant, while Joe was there, Claire had spent evenings with him. During her pregnancy, she stayed home with Finn. She spent mornings at the dumptique, Joe wrote and revised, and Finn went to the *Post*. It suited them all and everyone was content with a seemingly normal life.

Then, one warm fragrant night, Claire went into labor. Joe and Finn drove her to the hospital and hours later I was born.

Years later, Claire said, "How happy we were, the three happiest people in the world." And so they appeared to the Pequod community, a domesticated threesome, except it wasn't three: once I arrived, the three became four.

I'm sure my mother loved me but I never knew if her love sprang from a maternal instinct or out of desperation. She wanted it to be four and she tried, Claire tried hard, but she couldn't manage, she didn't know how, so it was three, that was the original plan and how it would be.

◯◯◯

I AM TOLD MY FATHER'S HAPPIEST HOURS WERE DURing Claire's pregnancy. The day I was born he announced, "Joely is my successor, my heir, the one to keep up the tradition of the *Post*."

From the time I could read, which was early, since both Finn and Joe coached me, I was my father's little copygirl and assistant. Other children played on weekends and vacations, but I helped Dad at the paper. There was a continual flow of winter people, summer people, fishermen discussing the tides, farmers predicting the weather, subscribers complaining their paper was late.

This was my life and I thought it was normal. Finn, a cigar dangling from his mouth, reading galleys, setting type, or working late and coming home exhausted. There was constant talk of expenses, ways to increase production and circulation, schemes to find new advertisers, and if a machine took sick or broke down, Finn was like a country doctor, tinkering, adjusting, and somehow nursing it back to health.

The *Post* was my playground, a grown-up world of printer's ink and old presses, and when my father looked at me, I saw pride in his eyes, and when he said, "I couldn't manage without my Joely's help," it meant more to me than all the dolls in the world.

And so the years rolled on, my father puttering with his presses or being host to whoever came into the office, my mother coming and going, a camera dangling from her shoulder, Joe leaving or returning to Pequod, lending a needed hand if and when he was free.

And if the way we lived seemed strange to others, it wasn't strange to me. From early childhood, I was aware our lives were different from anyone else's.

There would be a letter my mother carelessly left lying around, a saddened look on my father's face, the way Claire looked at Joe with eyes that said, I love you; the hearsay, the wisps of gossip that sink into your consciousness and become a sort of sixth sense.

Yes, the way we lived seemed strange to the good folk of Pequod, but it wasn't strange to me. It was childhood, adolescence, and all I ever knew.

I WAS THE ONE SHE TALKED TO, MY MOTHER'S CONFI-
dante. Claire didn't disguise how she felt or what had
happened—perhaps she wasn't able to—but talked about
my father and Joe as if I had been a witness to their
alliance. Yet, as much as she told me, I always felt she was
preoccupied by something else. She'd start a sentence,
throw me a knowing look—"I know I'm being indis-
creet, that there are things better left unsaid, things a
mother shouldn't tell a daughter"— and she'd continue,
embellishing her story with a new twist or revelation.
There! It was done! The unburdening of a guilty heart.
She was suddenly gay, and smiled, a smile that said, You
see! It's no longer important.

When my father was present, he was silent or turned
away. *To have, to hold, and, when necessary, let go!* That
was the contract he'd made in exchange for my mother,
who now, in some small measure, had become his
property.

I make it sound as if Claire sold herself into a kind of
bondage but it wasn't like that, not really; it was simply a
contract she'd entered into in order to be with a man who
obsessed her every waking hour, a man she felt to be her
soul mate, a man who wasn't really there.

My father felt a deep affection for me, but what he felt

for my mother was binding, blinding; Finn was a man in thrall. If he came into the room and Claire was holding me, the look in his eyes—how can I describe it?—was one of desperation, as if he wanted to grab me from her arms and jump into them himself.

Claire felt it too, for after a while, the normal physical affection a mother ordinarily shows a child was reserved for our hours alone. She once told me, "My old teacher, Eugene, warned me about the curse of an aching heart. Finn pretends he's happy, but I look into his eyes and I only see despair. I wanted the security of a family. And I wanted romantic love. I'm afraid your mother's too greedy, a little girl who's always hungry, a grown-up girl in search of a sweet."

After dark, when Claire would return from being with Joe, she'd come into my room and sit beside me on the bed.

"Are you asleep?" she'd whisper. If I said no, she'd kiss me and begin her story. If I said, "Momma, I'm sleeping," she'd laugh and say, "But who will I talk to if I don't talk to you?"

Year after year, through childhood and adolescence, my mother bared her soul. It didn't matter if I understood, what mattered was the telling, the clearing of her conscience, and since I was Claire's best friend, her ongoing tale became a lifelong confession.

My mother's confidences were intimate and uncensored, and I've often wondered if this was her way of turning me into an accomplice who would never accuse or confront her in later years. It was a lot to ask of a daughter, but I was hungry for mother love and this was my mother's way of loving me, so from my earliest years, I was Claire's captive audience.

One night I couldn't sleep. Neither could Finn, who came into my room and read to me until Claire came home. Then he stood, said, "Good night, sweet girl," and left us alone.

"Hello, Momma. I missed you."

"I was out chasing a moonbeam," she said. "Up and down and around the island, but whenever I got close, it rushed away. It sounds foolish, I know, but a moonbeam is magic, and whoever catches it, catches the magic. One day, he'll tire of the chase, and then it's mine, all mine, all the magic, mine."

"Why do you call it *he?* Like magic's a man?"

She laughed again, as if I had discovered an important truth, kissed me good night, and went off to be with Finn.

⌘

In THE BEST AND WORST OF MARRIAGES, INCLUDING the limited arrangement agreed upon by my parents, there are restrictions on the kind of freedom that allowed

Claire to pass from my father to Joe and back again to Finn.

It wasn't that they quarreled; it would be hard to quarrel with a man as even-tempered as my father, but more and more, despite his good nature, Finn was irritated by Claire's mood swings, her disappearance at night, her tardiness in coming home.

But she came back, she always came home, sat beside me, talked, and eventually went into their bedroom.

If Finn was sleeping, Claire would lie in the dark and replay the erotic hours she'd had with Joe. If Finn was shamming, pretending a half sleep, he was soon aroused and anxious to have her for himself.

"I imagine he's Joe," she confided. "Joe's arms around me, Joe's body in mine, and I wonder if it doesn't add to Finn's excitement, a kind of sexual stimulant that I come to him from his best friend's bed. But Finn continues to love me and says his love is unconditional. He says it is the reason our arrangement is manageable. Except it isn't. Something's happened. I don't know what, but Finn has changed, become victim to emotions that frighten him. I try to be honest, talk about the way I feel, but Finn denies or represses his anger. Or he changes the subject. So I close my eyes, I think of Joe, and Finn takes whatever I have left. We keep on with the pretense of sex as a part of a marital agreement or barter, and if it is emotional deception, it is the only way Finn can deal with what he said he wanted to have."

Claire paused and said, "I know you're wondering

why I stay with Finn. Why, it's simple. It's the only way I can be with Joe, or," she said ruefully, "that Joe will be with me."

Joe WAS GONE FOR LONGER PERIODS OF TIME AND Claire felt lost without him.

"Finn took good care of me and I was grateful," she said. "But when we made love, I thought of Joe, and the illusion of Joe's body filled me with desire. I found I was letting go with an ease and abandon I had once thought impossible. But when Joe came home, I couldn't be with both of them. I had managed before, but now, well, being with husband and lover wasn't part of our arrangement. The plan was to be with either Finn or Joe, not splitting myself between husband and lover on the same night.

"One night, alone with Finn, I let out a moan, except it wasn't a moan, it was Joe's name. I prayed Finn hadn't heard, but I opened my eyes and saw he was livid, his eyes wild with excitement, not the excitement of a man in his passion, but of a man betrayed. All Finn's pent-up rage and jealousy obliterated the sweet face of the man I married. Finn took a breath and tried to smile, as if a smile would calm him, restore him, but it didn't calm me, for it wasn't a smile, it was the grimace of a man out of control. It was time to be honest, Finn with me, and me with

Finn, so I said, 'The three of us, this triangle, was your idea. You insisted on it, said you could handle it, but you can't. You know it, I know it, and we've got to deal with what's happening.'

"'You're right, Claire, it's time we faced the truth.'

"I thought my words restored him but I was wrong.

"'There was a time I thought I could share you but I didn't count on, well, jealousy. I've tried to separate myself from it, believe me, Claire, I've tried, but it's like a tapeworm, gnawing inside me, chewing me up, and I see only one way out.'

"'What, Finn? Tell me the way.'

"'I know how you feel about Joe, and I know I can't lose you, so I've decided to talk to him, tell him everything, say I made a mistake, it's not working, and I can't go on. I'll leave it up to Joe. Joe will make the decision.'

"'You're being cruel.'

"'I'm saving our marriage.'

"I controlled my anger. Ridiculous as it seems, Joe and Finn were still at their boyhood game of two knights and a damsel in distress, and I knew Joe was too steadfast and loyal to ever marry me, so I was determined to win back Finn's trust and goodwill.

"'Yes,' I said. 'Let's be honest and admit the odds are against us. But let's ignore the odds, Finn. We're in too deep and can't go back. You say you love me, but do you? If you really love me, you'll accept I can't give Joe up. Oh, Finn, don't make me suffer any more than I have. The three of us love each other. Let's not hurt each other. Our mistake was in forgetting we're human. And vulnerable. If we put our hearts into making it work, it will, I know it will; we'll make it work.'

"And Finn believed me. I saw it in his eyes, and naïvely, I believed it too.

"And I tried," she said. "I stopped censoring myself and without a thought of my pleasure, I thought only of Finn's, for I needed his love. Finn was my rock, my haven, the father of my child. It's true, I'm greedy for love, and I could blame it on an unhappy childhood, but it's something more, something primal, as if I have two Claires inside me. One Claire wants domesticity, a husband and child, the other Claire rages with passion. Oh, Joely, can you ever understand? I've got two souls in one body, two warring souls who give me no peace."

As always, I was under Claire's spell, and yes, I was beginning to understand. My mother wanted motherhood but didn't want the responsibility of being a mother. I knew she wanted to love me but she only had love enough for Joe. I also knew what was really happening. If Claire was torn by love and guilt, so was I, a girl who wanted mother love, a daughter in love with her mother's lover.

"Tell me you do, Joely, say you love and forgive me."

"I love you," I said, but I didn't love her the way Claire wanted. With all my heart I wished I did.

IN THE MIDDLE OF THE ISLAND, A GENERAL STORE SELLS a hodgepodge of sundries, fresh fruit and vegetables, canned goods and hardware, fishing gear and birdseed. It serves as a post office for the more rural areas, and on Wednesday afternoon, the owner gives haircuts.

When Joe was on the island, he picked me up, filled the car with gas, and we drove to the dump. Claire never came along. She said it held too many bad memories, and she would go there only to work.

Joe loaded up on supplies, bought us sandwiches and Cokes, and we sat on a wooden bench on the porch and watched the people come and go. Everyone knew Joe and stopped to talk about the weather or the tides. When we finished eating, we got into his car and drove around the island.

Joe was like a walking history book. He said Pequod's history is not only of whaling men and their expeditions, but a history of flora and fauna, the great trees of the Northeast.

"Trees," he said, "are like people. They come from an ancient lineage. We can tell by the fossils."

"What's that? A fossil."

"A fossil is any trace of plant or animal life from an extinct geological time that's preserved in the earth's crust. Am I clear?"

"Not really."

"Well, millions of years ago, Pequod was covered with forests. These great trees were engulfed by the sea, and whales and sharks swam over the buried land. Then, a sheet of ice flowed down from the north. It was known as the Ice Age, and lasted until the climate warmed. The sun melted the glaciers and raised the level of the sea. That's when Pequod became an island. The great survivors are the trees, the pines and sassafras, the olives and oaks. Trees are the true Pequod historians."

"Even Mom's old oak?"

"That old fellow may well hold all the secrets of the island."

"If you love Pequod so much, why do you leave?"

"Not important. What is important is I always return."

"Because of the trees?"

"And the sea and the sky. Because it's my history. Because I can't stay away."

He didn't mention Claire, but I knew she was on his mind.

We canoed on the Great Pond and walked on the beaches and Joe taught me how to swim. I draped strands of seaweed over his shoulders, called him my seaweed man, and I loved him; with each passing year, I loved him even more.

When Claire joined us, we drove to her old oak. Joe lay on the ground with his head in her lap and she touched his face and whispered to him, and when it was safe, when my attention was elsewhere, she bent her head and kissed him.

In the evening, we sat around the old wooden table. My father talked about the *Post,* Joe talked about his book, and my mother joked about me.

"Joely's got a crush on you, Joe," she said, very matter-of-fact.

"Mother, don't!"

"It's only normal, darling girl. A lovestruck adolescent and a handsome man."

"I'm not lovestruck."

"Of course you're not! Just remember, Joely, it's only a crush and you'll grow out of it."

"Did you grow out of it?" I wanted to say, but I was silent, for even then I knew I mustn't react. I knew Claire couldn't share Joe with any other human being. Particularly me. My job was to be a dutiful daughter, to listen, be loyal, and remain silent.

IT WAS ALWAYS THE SAME.

The day Joe was to leave, my mother was brusque, her mood swings ominous as the sky before a storm, and lasting until a letter arrived with the date of his return.

. . .

It was sunny that day, the day Joe was due home, and my mother said I could join her at the dock, so we waited for him to walk down the ramp.

When others were around, Joe seemed amused by my mother's obvious infatuation, but when they were alone, that is, alone with me, they were silent. On the dock that morning, uncharacteristically, Joe put his arm around Claire's waist, and I felt a shiver pass between them.

"If I hold you one more second, I won't pull away," he said.

But he did pull away, and driving back to his place, Claire said, "Since you're not going to marry me, what are you going to do with me?"

"Let's discuss it later."

"No, Joe, I want to talk about it now."

"I'll be with you. The way we are. The way we'll keep on being."

"Except it's not working. Admit it, Joe, we're stuck in a dead end."

"This isn't the time."

"Joely knows, she knows everything. And so does Finn. He never raises his voice, but he's resentful and angry, and one day it will turn to rage."

"I said not now."

She glanced at me through the rearview mirror. Our eyes met and then she focused on the road.

"I love you too much, it's my tragic flaw."

"Why are you turning this into a melodrama?"

"It's how I feel."

"Well, it isn't. So don't."

"What is it, then?"

"The three of us, bound together, responsible to each other, and that is not high drama."

Claire was silent. She stopped the car in front of his house and Joe opened the door and got out.

Through the open window she said, "Some women are lucky. They're only jealous of other women."

"I'll see you and Finn for dinner, and for God's sake, no theatrics."

"I'll behave."

Joe waved at me, picked up his suitcase, and walked to the door.

⟨℞⟩

EVERYONE SO SILENT, UNNERVING, THE SILENCE HANG-ing over our house until, one night, Claire snapped.

"This tension's unbearable. You're punishing me, Finn, and I don't deserve it."

"I'm not doing anything."

"Then why so silent? So disapproving? Why do I feel like judge and jury are passing sentence on my life?"

"You're overreacting."

"Am I? I don't think so. Something's wrong and you won't face it."

My father, who masked his emotions with a laugh or a smile, stopped smiling.

"What's wrong is when the phone rings, you think it's him. If there's the sound of footsteps, you jump to attention, as if you're waiting for him. What's wrong is when I kiss you, you're not with me. You haven't been for years."

"So I must pay a price."

"You asked me what's wrong. Well, now you know."

"What's wrong, what's really wrong, is you won't face the reason I married you. I love you, Finn, but like a sister for a brother. I never promised you great love and you said it didn't matter, said you could handle it, and I believed you, and so we were married. It wasn't about who loves who the most, or the ringing of the phone, or the sound of a footstep. It was about accepting me as I am. I know you try, Finn. You wish you could, but you can't. You're angry with me, jealous of Joe, and I'm sick and tired of feeling like a criminal."

Finn looked at me and said, "I'm sorry you have to hear about our problems this way, Joely, but I'm sure you've got a good idea of what's going on."

Then, looking at Claire, he said, "Up until now, I've been able to deal with our situation because the woman I love told me, in her limited way, she loved me too, but you're right, Claire, something's changed, something has gone wrong."

"The girl you fell in love with was begging on street corners, and I've wondered so often, was it love you felt for me or pity?"

"How can you ask that? Oh, Claire, don't you remember saying, 'We're human, all of us, vulnerable'?"

"I remember."

"Then allow me my vulnerability as I allow you yours."

Finn went to the window and looked into the street. When he turned and faced us, you could see a change in his eyes. The scene was played out, it was over, and once again the eyes said, I am in charge of my emotions. "I'm taking an oath," he said. "No more grand passion, no jealous scenes. I promise to act in a civilized way, and our lives can go on, just like before."

That night, Claire came to my room, sat beside me, and said, "Poor deluded Finn. He means what he says, every word, but how can you be civilized about passion when its very meaning defies civility? It's a ridiculous oath, but Finn's determined to make our marriage work. He'll bury his anger, at least for now, and think he's safe. You can see my dilemma, Joely, how torn I am. I may not be in love with Finn, but I cherish his golden heart and I can't violate his one small hope of happiness. I once told him that even though the odds were against us, we could beat the odds, and I meant it. But I don't know, I don't know how long any of us can hang on."

Despite my mother's confidences, I never felt her to have a normal maternal instinct, yet it was there, in her pictures of the dump, a scavenging child, a girl clutching a broken doll, children playing in the ruins, all the sympathy and concern a mother feels for a child.

One afternoon, beneath the tree that brought her luck, Claire showed her pictures to Joe.

"Promise you'll be honest. More important, promise you'll be kind."

"How kind shall I be?"

"And don't tease."

One by one Joe studied the photographs. "They're simple, Claire, emotional, and haunting."

"You really like them?"

"You've caught a world of childhood loneliness and want."

"I wasn't sure what I wanted. Then, one gray day, I saw a girl picking through the junk, and I had the strangest feeling, as if I knew her, really knew her, and in that second I also knew nothing has changed, the girl of my childhood is still with me, like a shadow, but now I don't want to run, Joe, I want to face that world I've always fled."

"Quite a discovery. Finding you can't run from who you are."

"But the miracle, the real discovery, is when I lift my camera to my eye and shoot, it's gone, all the loneliness, the shame, and I know that if I can capture the harsh world of my childhood, I'll finally find peace."

Joe took her hand and kissed it.

"And you, Joe, you've always pulled away, said you couldn't hurt Finn, and I've gone along with it. But that's over. I love you, and you won't admit it, but you love me too. You're my true husband. I'm your true wife."

"You're too much of a romantic," Joe said and released her hand. "Why can't you understand? I'm protecting us both from the kind of desire that makes a normal life impossible."

"I don't want protection from who I am."

"But I do."

"You're lying, and it's too late for lies. This time, when you leave Pequod, I'm coming too."

"You'd distract me. I wouldn't get any work done, and that, my lovely friend, is the price you pay for being so beautiful."

"You're still lying. At least to yourself. The truth is you feel guilty about Finn, and your guilty conscience is ruling your life."

"And Joely. What about Joely?"

"If I was a man on assignment, Joely wouldn't be an issue."

"Be reasonable, Claire."

"It's too late to be reasonable."

That moment, my mother lifted her mouth, and the touch of her lips was like an earthquake on his nervous system. Joe knew whatever he said, wherever he went, however long he stayed away, Claire was part of him. He knew he'd never pull free.

❦

I'M NOT SURE WHOSE IDEA IT WAS, BUT ONE NIGHT, sitting around the table looking at Claire's pictures, my father said, "You've captured it! The grim life of children who have known little else but poverty."

"These kids are a microcosm of poor kids everywhere," said Joe. "They've learned about survival the way other kids learn their ABCs. The brutal statistic is one out of four children in America lives in poverty."

"I know what hunger is. That's what I want to show," said Claire.

Finn was thoughtful.

"There have been studies on hunger in America, on poverty in America, but has anyone focused a camera on American children living in a culture of poverty? That's the book, Claire, the book you were meant to do."

"You're serious, Finn, I mean really serious?"

"I know you can do it!"

Claire knew Finn was telling her she had his okay, that

he supported the idea of her going on assignment, that he was giving her his blessing to go away with Joe. Finn was releasing her from the responsibility of being mother and wife. If jealousy had driven love away, Finn's instinct for survival revived it.

"But the final decision is Joe's."

The two men regarded each other in silence. Then Joe smiled.

"Well, I guess I've got a collaborator."

"It's settled," said Finn.

Claire was luminous. She stood and went to Finn, and her kiss, the feel of her mouth on his cheek, restored the illusion that the three of them could return to where they had started, that what had begun as a circle of love would continue on its arc.

A FLURRY OF ACTIVITY, PLANS MADE, PLANS REVISED, Joe writing a proposal, appointments with agents, talks with publishers, and finally a contract. The day had come. Apprehensive and excited, Joe and Claire were ready to go.

Claire had spent a childhood being charming and seductive, and charm, for my mother, was like a second skin, so whatever qualms she may have had about leaving me behind, she disguised with a smile.

"This is Finn's idea, darling, an opportunity I can't pass up."

"I'll miss you," I said.

"And I'll miss my Joely, but every day, at five o'clock, I'll think of you, you think of me, and it will be as if we're kissing."

"I'll still miss you."

"Remember we once rented a video called *The Red Shoes*? Remember how the girl had to dance, that nothing could stop her? I'm like that girl. Try to understand why she did what she did and you'll know why I'm going and forgive me."

"I remember she danced into the sea."

My mother laughed. "Don't be afraid, darling, I love you too much to do anything that would hurt either of us."

And I believed her, believed my mother loved me, believed her love was strong enough to protect us both from danger or harm.

◈

Joe, HARDWORKING AND INTENSELY FOCUSED, LIKED to rise early and be out by eight. Claire watched him work, unobtrusive, sympathetic, easily drawing out the kids, and writing in a notebook or recording their voices on a small machine.

"It's about trust," he said. "About winning their confidence and trusting your own emotions and instinct."

Claire was an apt student. She was slow, patient, didn't seem to study her subjects and made them unaware of the camera. When they accepted her presence, she closed in and took her picture. She asked questions, wrote down what she heard with a precise detail for each shot. She smiled and charmed—it was her way—hid whatever she felt under a blank expression.

"As a child, I learned to make my face a blank. It was how I dealt with my mother's drunken rages. I smiled, didn't threaten anyone, and no one knew what I felt. When I begged, people saw a lovable girl who fate had dealt a dirty hand and gave me more money than they ordinarily would have. Being invisible: I used it as a child, I use it now. I turn it on and get the picture I want."

Within weeks, Joe was confident Claire could do the interviews without him. He spent his days writing while she took her camera and went out alone.

She slipped in and out of gender, one day dressed as a woman, the next as a man. The children clustered around her, disclosed the most intimate details of their lives, and begged her to take their picture. It was like a Pied Piper's convention and Claire promised to send each child a photograph.

When she returned to Joe, she showed him her notes. "We've got a lot of individual stories," he said. "Now our job's to weave them into a common theme."

They traveled from town to town and state to state. Claire photographed children living in tenements, working in fields, children in rags, without shoes, or passing shoes between them. She shot pregnant teenage girls, boys in gangs, children without hope, at the mercy of hunger and disease and living in fantasies of rage and revenge.

"I know what their lives will be because they don't have a chance," she said. "If I can photograph the danger and pain, our work can do some good."

In the evening they made love.

One night, Joe pulled free of her arms. "Why couldn't I find a normal woman?" he groaned, but smiled.

"How can I be normal when it's like a force of nature?"

She pulled him down, whispered obscenities, and the touch of his fingers, the feel of his mouth, his tongue inside her, the long slow thrust and warm sweet heat, spreading and spilling over: She could bear it no longer. She clung to his body. He didn't pull free.

⁂

As long as I remember, I helped out at the paper. Now I was to be Finn's bona fide assistant. And alone with my father, I saw him escalate his martinis. He didn't drink steadily or pass out dead drunk, but on Sundays he'd go on a bender. Yet Monday morning, despite headache or hangover, my father, smiling and convivial, was always back at work.

Until this time, Finn had been silent about his marriage, but once he'd belted down the gin, the gin began to talk, and once the gin was talking, Finn seemed unable to stop.

"Your mother's right. I do drink too much, but gin's not the problem. The problem is my heart, the way she looks at him with those gooey in-love eyes, and when she leaves my bed to go to his, it's more than a normal man can bear. I swallow the hurt, I bury it deep, but I can't turn it off, and the hurt gets worse, and all my selfless intentions seem like a farce. Claire says this torment's ridiculous, says I should get her out of my system with another woman. Maybe she's right. I tell you, Joely, I'd give my eyeteeth to let her go, but she's like a fire in my brain. I look at her, smell her, hear her voice, and I can't let go. I watch her pacing back and forth, like a caged animal, restless, about to explode, and I jumped at the idea of her going with Joe."

There's such a look of sadness in my father's eyes. I've seen him depressed but never like this.

"You love her that much?"

"She's like an illness that's got hold of my soul, and if I'm a fool, I know these modern ideas come with a price. I have no choice. I can't bear to have Claire out of my sight, much less lose her, but if I want to keep her, I must let her go."

<hr>

R ESEARCH FINISHED, PHOTOGRAPHS TAKEN, JOE AND Claire came home. Joe shut himself in his house and my mother complained.

"You know I need privacy when I work," he said.

"And I distract you."

"Yes, you distract me."

"Yet you managed to work when we were on the road."

"We're no longer on the road."

"I hope you enjoy what you're doing."

"I enjoy my work, if that's what you mean."

"I mean closing the door on our life."

"I don't want to hurt you but this is how it's got to be."

"If you're apologizing, I accept."

"It's whatever you want to call it."

Claire smiled the smile that had once brought her dollars instead of small change.

"I'll consider it an apology, so expect me this evening around eight."

COMMUNICATION BETWEEN MY FATHER AND JOE WAS at a standstill. Once close as brothers, now they were silent. Joe came to the house for dinner on Saturday nights, but the banter was gone, the old camaraderie; conversation was awkward and forced.

My father, so focused on running the paper, was confused by what was happening. He and Claire had gone through difficult times, but there was a new edge to the way she distanced herself. The agreement was if Joe was on the island, she would go to him for a few hours at night, and however Finn felt, he was not neglected, for Claire played with him and made him happy.

It was obvious she didn't feel the same rapture for him she felt for Joe, but Finn continued to believe she loved him, that it was more than mere affection, and he treasured her endearments and caresses.

"Claire's not a boyhood folly I would have ordinarily outgrown," he told me. "She's my great weakness. Your mother's my Achilles' heel."

One morning over breakfast, we heard her, step by step, very slowly, coming down the stairs. She opened the coat closet, and Finn rose from the table and went to her side.

"Going out?"

"Yes, I'm going out."

"A morning walk will do you good."

"Wouldn't that be nice."

"No need for sarcasm."

But before he finished, she opened the door and closed it.

Finn returned to the kitchen. I saw how distracted he was and poured him a cup of coffee. He sipped it without speaking.

Unexpectedly, the front door opened. It was Claire.

"I hate it when I'm moody. Tell me you forgive me."

My father looked like a man lost at sea, and Claire was the beacon to guide him back to shore.

"We're only human and sometimes not in charge of our feelings," he said. "But I know things will work out. I'll do my damnedest to make sure they do."

Claire bent over, gently kissed him, and in a barely audible voice said, "I'm impossible to live with, I know it, Finn, but you're my dearest, most trusted friend, and if I take you for granted, forgive me, darling. I won't do it anymore."

My father looked as if he wanted to fling himself at her feet in a show of slavish devotion, but a ferry blast interrupted whatever he was going to say, so he looked at his watch and said instead, "I'm late. I'd better get to the office."

"Thanks for being so patient."

"What's best for all of us, Claire, is to forget our troubles with work. Work's the answer, the only cure."

"Yes, Finn."

"And remember, I'm the guy who wanted this arrangement, and I'm strong enough to deal with it."

"Yes, Finn."

"And if you've got time, I can use an extra pair of hands at the paper."

"Emergency?"

"Not an emergency."

"Then not today."

He didn't seem upset. "Well, Joely, how about it?"

"Sure, Daddy, I'll be there after school."

I knew my mother wanted a serious talk, so that night, when she came into my room, I was ready to listen.

"This morning after I left, I drove to my tree. I weighed all the reasons why I married Finn, like a scale, on the one hand this, on the other hand that. I thought about my childhood and the importance of safety. I thought of Finn's love and kindness, his offer of protection. I knew Joe would never hurt or betray him, so Finn's idea of sharing me seemed inspired, a way of having security and of being with Joe. And I thought about you, Joely, and how strange and difficult it's been for you, so I've decided to postpone any decision I will one day face, because I want my daughter to have a normal day-to-day life."

"Normal? You think our life is normal?"

"Under the circumstances, I do. Finn and I have done everything we could to keep it like that."

"Do you know what you're saying?"

But Claire was into her story, so I decided to postpone what one day would be an unpleasant confrontation.

". . . I walked to the cliffs," she said. "Watched the clouds changing shape, and the waves and the sky. I thought about love, how love has defined me, how it's molded and given shape to my life, and I thought, I'm still a lovestruck girl, a half-child, a half-woman, and in that moment I knew I must become a mature grown-up before I make any decisions."

"What kind of decisions?"

"I'm not exactly sure. Something, a change." Claire was suddenly shy. "Do you understand how much I want to grow up, and that I may need your help?"

"I'm here."

"My darling girl."

It was one of the few times my mother seemed involved in my existence. Claire smiling, Claire talking to me as if we were the only two people in the world. It was her smile, the way she touched your hand, how her eyes looked into yours that gave you a feeling of absolute intimacy. She did it with Finn, she did it with Joe, and tonight she did it with me. It was Claire's unspoken declaration of unconditional love. It lasted a second but was engraved on your soul for the rest of your life.

JOE WAS LIVING LIKE A HERMIT. HE LEFT HIS HOUSE to go on errands or make an occasional trip to Cambridge. Claire asked who he was seeing and he said, "I'm not ready to talk about it, but when I am, you'll be the first to know."

"You're not being honest."

"And you're being jealous."

"Jealous of who? Who am I jealous of?"

"Jealous of *whom*. I'll tell you when I'm ready!"

A few weeks passed and Joe called to say he had finished the book and was inviting himself over for a celebratory dinner. Claire said to come on Sunday night. She cooked her specialty, a brisket of beef it took two days to prepare. Sunday afternoon, the phone rang.

"I feel awful calling at this late hour, but I'm completely wiped out and all I want is to collapse on my bed. Will you forgive me, Claire? Can we postpone our dinner another week?"

"But I've cooked a brisket, the way you love it, swimming in vermouth."

"Freeze it."

"Then let me come to you."

"I've got to sleep, Claire, and I've got to be in Cambridge early Monday. Be a good girl. Say you forgive me."

Claire laughed. "Only because I love you."

"I know," he said softly, and hung up.

A wind had come up and a sudden hard rain. The doorbell rang and my mother sprang to open it. Joe was wearing a trench coat. He looked like the hero of a Hemingway novel. Claire threw her arms around his chest and he disengaged from her embrace.

"Well, aren't you going to ask me in?"

"How about a drink?" said Finn from the living room, and filled a glass with scotch.

"Hey, easy on that stuff."

"Finn will finish off whatever you don't want."

Finn shot Claire a withering look. She disregarded it. "Okay," he said. "Time to disclose the reason for Cambridge."

Joe swallowed his drink. "I'll start with background data. This is important, Claire, so please don't interrupt."

"Me? Interrupt?"

Finn finished his drink and poured himself another. Claire looked at him but kept silent.

Joe said, "As early as the 1930s, scientific researchers discovered a group of synthetic compounds that suppressed plant growth. It seemed a blessing, particularly to the farmer in his relentless war against weeds. Then, during World War Two, safer, more powerful herbicides were created, and once the war was over, these various compounds were tested for commercial use, and research was accelerated."

"Yes," said Claire, "but what about Cambridge?"

"Didn't you promise not to interrupt?"

"My lips are sealed."

"In the sixties, when we were at war with Vietnam, the president approved an air strategy of low-flying planes dropping a mixture of chemicals over South Vietnam's land areas. These chemicals were known as Agent Orange, and were part of a family of compounds called dioxins, used to destroy crops and defoliate forests. Scientists claim Agent Orange was the most toxic, deadliest molecule ever synthesized by man.

"Aerial spraying continued for five years. I'll skip the hundreds upon thousands of tragic stories of dying veterans exposed to the toxic horror. Finally, the National Cancer Institute issued a report on the hazards. A Harvard scientist managed to get hold of a copy, and the Pentagon could no longer suppress the danger."

"Our next book," said Claire. I saw her throw a look at Finn. But Joe ignored her and continued.

"We live in a time of technical revolution. For decades, we've been developing new industrial processes. Synthetic chemicals emerge from our laboratories that involve new patterns of consumption and destruction. These innovations profit society, but they also create new risks and dangers, and that's the tragic paradox, that what began as a great hope for a technical revolution benefiting society has brought with it the insidious danger of tumors, birth abnormalities, damage to the organs . . . well, the list goes on and on. The ghastly contradiction is human ingenuity has created human suffering, a risk to water and food supplies, a time bomb to the environment, and affecting all living creatures, not only ourselves, but our children and our children's children for generations to come. Well, my research has led me to MIT and Harvard scientists, and the message I get is we've made a Faustian bargain with the chemical world. That's what I'm going to investigate, this bargain we've made with the devil."

"So that's the reason for Cambridge," said Claire.

"That's it."

"We'll do it together, Joe, expose it together."

"Look, Claire, I want to get one thing straight. I am not going to collaborate. Can you understand? This time I work alone."

The rain had stopped. The living room window was open.

"I love the rain," said Claire. "The rain calms me."

"Get back to work and you won't need calming," said Joe.

"I wouldn't need calming if I came along with you."

"I thought I made myself clear."

Claire was silent, then blurted out, "Why are you so selfish?"

"My so-called selfishness has never bothered you before."

"Hasn't it?"

"What Joe means is—" Finn interrupted.

"I know what he means," said Claire, her voice cool and crisp. "What you mean, Joe, is I'm a threat to your peace of mind so you think you'll escape me by running away. And you, Finn, you think tucking me into a safe little crib will protect me from my outrageous passion. Well, it doesn't, so stop it, both of you, stop treating me like a naughty child."

"I'm going alone. My mind is made up."

Claire stood by the window and looked into the dark. A sudden gust of wind tore through the room. It seemed to calm her, for when she closed the window and turned around, she was transformed from a rejected lover into a charming waif who smiled for your money and danced her way into your heart.

She came to my side and took my hand in hers.

"Pay no attention to us, Joely, we're just three children pretending to be grown up."

WHILE CLAIRE WAS GONE, FINN'S WEEKEND BINGES didn't interfere with his work, but Claire was home now, and his drinking disturbed her, so she lectured him and he laughed.

"I hurt no one, and it keeps me from the blues."

So Claire purred, she coaxed and cajoled, and Finn promised to stop, and he did, for a while, he stopped and was his old solicitous self, so it was unusual to see him lose control, as he did one day when he asked to see Claire's recent pictures.

"I have no new pictures, Finn, nothing to show you."

"Not a single one?"

"Not a single one."

"And may I ask why not?"

"Of course you may ask and the answer is simple. I want to live life, not take pictures of it. I don't want to pretend taking a picture is living a life."

"And what do you mean by living a life?"

"Living my life. Why, it was a promise made me before we were married."

"I think I've upheld my part of the bargain."

"Have you? The bargain was about freedom, that was our bargain, but it's turned out to be a lie, a lie I couldn't face, so I've pulled it around me, tighter and tighter, buried myself in it until I feel like its prisoner."

"I think I understand. You see yourself as a prisoner of a lie."

"You said I'd be free, that we'd be happy, all of us, but we're not, Finn, we're in limbo, hanging in space, and that's not how I want to spend the rest of my life."

"Do you know what I think, Claire? That your over-developed imagination blinds you to the fact of the real cause of your unhappiness, that Joe wouldn't marry you. I offered you marriage, as well as a crack at high romance, and you grabbed it. The truth is Joe doesn't want you tagging along, and my sorrow is you don't see you've got everything you want, a husband, a lover, and Joely."

My mother looked at me as if I'd been buried for years and was suddenly excavated. I wanted her to say something tender or loving, but she said, "This must be painful to hear, Joely, but it's time you knew the truth."

"I know the truth!"

"Of course you do." Then, as some sort of afterthought, "Oh, Joely, tell your mother you love her."

But I couldn't do it, couldn't say "I love you" so Claire would be happy. She had love enough from my father and Joe. I was a repository, that was my job, to be a safe-deposit box for Claire's secret life, and I was playing by her rules. I suppose I loved my mother, I knew how much she wanted it, but Claire wanted everyone's love, and by now I knew I wanted love too.

JOE WAS GONE FOR A MONTH. A LETTER FINALLY arrived, and Claire drove to her tree, sat under the branches, and committed every word to memory. Joe was coming home, a matter of days.

"We'll meet him together," I said.

"Sorry, Joely, not this time."

"Why not?"

"Because I want to meet him alone."

The day of Joe's return, Claire wore a yellow sweater that gave her eyes an amber cast. She looked very beautiful. She left the house and returned after dark.

She came into my room that night, the room of her confessor, the one to absolve her of her guilt, and what I understood was irrelevant, what mattered was the telling, that I was an innocent ear and not a voice of judgment.

And as she talked, I thought, I'm as guilty as you, perhaps even more, for I love Joe too.

Did she know what I was thinking? How could she not, smiling in that way of hers, saying, "Joe's too handsome for his own good. You look into his deep gray eyes and think you've found your destiny, but destiny is tricky, it works in unexpected ways. . . ."

"What unexpected ways?"

"My poor Joely," she said and laughed. "I'm afraid you've inherited your mother's romantic nature, but remember, crushes don't last. A nice young man will come along and Joe will be forgotten."

She continued to smile, and I fell under her spell. I always fell under my mother's spell, but when I came to my senses, the spell had worn off.

One night she leaned over and kissed me. "You smell like flowers," I said.

"Not flowers, Joely, happiness. I finally found the courage to say I can't go on. I said Finn's repressed every feeling, but the anger's there, and one day it will explode. Oh, Joely, you can't imagine what it's like, this waltz from Finn to Joe and back again to Finn. Joe suffers, Finn suffers, and I suffer, and tonight I said, 'If you love me at all, Joe, you won't send me home.'"

"What did he say?"

"He was silent at first. Then, in a soft careful voice, he said, 'Give me time, Claire. I promise it will be all right.'

"And miracle of miracles, his mask of detachment and remoteness was gone, and I knew he loved me; it was there, in his eyes."

Then Claire paused. "You can't imagine the times I've asked myself if love would have worked for me if I'd tried my luck from the beginning. But I didn't. I lived by Finn's rules, and Joe's, in a secret covert life. Oh, Joely, try and understand how much I love him. I love the way he moves and how he touches me, the feel of his mouth—"

"Don't tell me about your sex life. Not again. I don't want to know."

"One day you'll be grateful you haven't grown up in a shroud of secrecy and gossip."

"Why can't you understand? I'm your daughter and don't want to know."

She looked at me hard, as if she didn't recognize me, then she softened.

"If I talk too much, it's because you're the only one I trust. If that makes me unfit to be a mother, I plead guilty."

"I hate what you're doing!"

"What am I doing?"

"Don't you know?"

"If I knew I wouldn't ask."

"What you're doing, what you've always done, which is lay your guilt on me. What you're really guilty of is wanting motherhood without the responsibility of being a mother. Why did you get pregnant unless you thought having a child would somehow make it all work?"

Claire didn't flinch. Instead, she took my hand in hers.

"I know you think I love Joe more than you, but it's not so. I wanted a child. I loved the child inside me. You're a part of me, Joely, there's no one I love the way I love you."

She raised my hand to her lips, then kissed me on the mouth, stood, and went to her room.

CLAIRE HAD SPENT THE DAY IN BOSTON, AND WAS due on the five o'clock ferry. It was raining and dark, night coming on hard. Finn, home for an early supper, was returning to the office for a late night of work.

It was not in Finn's character to pry among Claire's belongings, but for some strange and unaccountable reason, he was rummaging through her files. The mystery is why Claire had left them unlocked, for it was here, in various unmarked manila folders, she kept her cache of secret pictures.

Whatever Finn's motive, I heard his shriek, and when I opened the door, he was unrecognizable, blinded by rage, tearing up her photographs of Joe, and scattering them. The look in his eyes was ominous, dark, a signal of danger. He caught me staring and managed to get hold of himself.

"From the beginning," he said, "Claire's bewitched me. I sound like a lunatic but it's so. 'Save yourself,' I tell myself, 'and let her go,' but it's my brain talking, not my heart. I've spent my life forgiving her, Joely, but it's gone, used up, finished, all the forgiveness in me. Look at your father! At the pathetic deteriorated mess I've become, as if an illness has rotted my soul . . ."

A church bell chimed. It chimed six times. A car pulled up in front of the house. Finn quickly poured a drink and swallowed. Claire opened the front door. She came inside and looked at the black-and-white fragments that littered the floor.

"Those pictures are for my eyes only. Private property. You had no right to destroy them."

It was as though Finn had planned in advance what he would say, for when he spoke, he was calm and his voice controlled.

"A husband's right, Claire, a naïve and idiotic husband who thought his love could compete with the sexual lure of his best friend's bed."

"I've never deceived you. You know I love Joe."

"Love! Is that what you call it? This feeding frenzy for a man who turns our life into a prison. Don't deny it. It's how you feel when you come back at night, like a prisoner returning to her jailer."

"Yes! It's how I feel!"

"My poor deprived wife. She travels with her lover, works with him, sleeps with him, and her deluded husband looks the other way while she ruins everyone's life."

"The only life I've ruined is my own."

"Spare me, please."

"I was young and confused and I made a pact with the devil. Well, I've danced with him and paid his price. Now I want to be free."

"I see. And when, may I ask, did this newfound wisdom strike?"

Finn poured another drink.

Claire smiled, the smile as fixed on her face as a newly minted coin.

"Getting drunk is not the answer."

"Maybe not but it helps."

"Can't we talk without rancor?"

"I've got to think, Claire." He reached into a pocket and pulled out a set of car keys.

"Please, Finn. Not in your condition."

"My condition is splendid."

"Then I'm coming with you."

Claire held out her hand, and like an obedient child,

Finn handed them over. She went into the front hall, pulled two slickers from a hook, held one up for Finn, and draped the other over her shoulder.

"You're right. A drive and fresh air will ease the tension and do us both good."

She opened the front door and closed it behind Finn. I went to the window and watched her drive into the night.

❧

IT STOPPED RAINING, AND SUDDENLY, SWIFTLY, STARTED again, lashing the windshield and flooding the road.

Claire would be driving very fast, ignoring the speedometer—that was her way behind the wheel of a car—and she would be talking, driving and talking, asking Finn for a divorce. He would protest, of course, but nothing would deter her, no argument or logic, no amount of pleading. My mother's mind was made up and she was determined. Finn would urge her to slow down and Claire would say, "I've been driving these roads all my life and I could drive them blindfolded."

Through lightning flash and burst of thunder they would argue, animated and angry, accusing and defending, when suddenly, zooming out of the dark and rushing at full gallop toward the sharp glare of headlights, would come a dark, unfocused blur.

"Dammit! What kind of idiot lets a dog loose on a night like this?"

Finn would grab the wheel from Claire's hand and turn it hard, as hard as it would go, but it was as if the car had taken over and was driving itself, veering off the road, jumping a ditch, skidding into a wooded field, and smashing against the trunk of an old oak.

Claire was pinned beneath the steering wheel. It was stuck in her chest but she was conscious. She could taste her blood and knew she was hurt. She started to cough and the pain got worse.

"Finn! . . . Finn! . . ."

But there was only silence.

"Finn . . . Are you all right? Finn . . . Answer me . . . Please . . ."

And more silence.

She felt tears on her face and knew she was crying. That's all she remembered, the taste of the blood and the salt of the tears. . . .

It didn't let up. The rain, the lightning, the crashes of thunder so loud I could hardly hear the ringing phone or a man's voice saying, "Miss Hurley?"

"I'm Miss Hurley."

"This is Officer Dann. I'm sorry to disturb you but there's been an accident."

"Oh God!"

"You'd better come right to the hospital, miss. I'll be here when you arrive."

WHEN I WENT INTO THE HOSPITAL ROOM, JOE WAS standing beside her. He excused himself and said he was going to talk to the doctor.

My mother looked so frail and small. I pulled up a chair and sat by the bed, but I didn't cry, not then. I wanted Claire to see me strong.

"Finn is dead," she said.

"It was raining hard, and dark."

"'It's a dog!' Finn cried, but it was too late. And now Finn is dead!" She paused. "And the dog? Is the dog dead too?"

"The dog ran away."

Claire shut her eyes.

"Are you in pain?"

She didn't answer.

"Before the end, before Finn went crazy, he was so nice to me. You don't know how nice Finn could be, and I was going to ask him for a divorce. And that's the awful irony because now I don't need it. Ridiculous, isn't it? One minute life is utterly real; it belongs to you and all you have to do is reach out and grab it. Then, suddenly, it's wrenched away."

"Oh, Momma."

"And all I want is to say Finn's name. To beg his forgiveness. More than anything in the world, I want Finn to forgive me."

I held back my tears, but once I started to cry, I couldn't stop. I held Claire's hand, kissed her palm, her fingers, and whispered, "Momma, Momma."

And in a barely audible voice she said, "I know, Joely, I feel it too, all the love between us, I feel it too."

CRS

A SERVICE WAS HELD IN THE PEQUOD TOWN HALL, and one by one, the townsfolk stood and spoke of Finn's kindness, his generosity and help when they were in trouble. Everyone was crying. Joe called Finn a spiritual brother, and in a faraway counterpoint, a dog began to howl.

Afterward, we buried Finn in the Seaman's Cemetery, but it didn't seem real, nothing seemed real, the weeping in the pews, the creaking of the schooners, the ominous howl of a faraway dog.

No, it didn't seem real. My father's sudden death, my mother's mangled body. Only Joe was real, organizing every detail and leading my mother and me, step-by-step, through our confusion and sorrow, as if we were children learning to walk.

Joe chartered a plane and we flew Claire to a hospital in Boston. She was operated on the following morning and regained consciousness by night.

"The doctor says she's out of danger, but her spine is badly damaged," said Joe.

"How badly?"

"Claire may never walk again."

"You can't mean . . ."

"I mean she's going to need all our care and attention and our undivided love."

"Then you're coming back to Pequod."

"We'll shut the *Post* for a couple of weeks. For an interim period, I'll run it with you."

"And afterward? What happens then?"

"It's your paper, Joely. Finn would have wanted you to run it, as you have been doing. I've saved money, and with an occasional freelance assignment, we'll be fine. As for Claire, she's too proud to complain, to hint at how she's really feeling, but if she begins to feel neglected or useless, she could slide into depression, and our job's to keep that from happening. The doctor assures me she's strong, in good enough physical condition to eventually go on crutches, and in the meantime she'll use a wheel-chair. My hope is she'll want to help out at the paper, and with encouragement, start to photograph again. We'll have to use everything in our power to make that happen, and I think she'll be all right."

Joe's face was close to mine, and if I felt breathless, I

felt no guilt, for I knew that if I loved him in silence, no one would know and no one would be hurt.

⁂

WITHOUT TEARS, ANGER, OR COMPLAINT, AND LIKE the New England stoic she was, Claire came to accept that the days of the jaunty wild girl in the boyish cap were over. From now on, her life would be circumscribed and limited, and she would be dependent upon others for most of her needs. And yet, she seemed undaunted. If her body was frail, her spirit was gay. She smiled, laughed, seemed almost lighthearted.

"I'm still in love with that smile," said Joe.

"Say it again."

"Crazy in love with a beautiful smile."

"I used to wonder, still do, if it's not an old bad habit, smiling in a quest for love. Perhaps I think it brings me luck. I smile. You react. You're moved. Think I'm pretty. And brave. You start to love me and love protects me from my fear. I used to wake up with it, like a hang-over, but since the accident, it's lifted. Isn't it strange how I've found hope. . . . Why, Joe, you're trembling. Are you cold?"

"I'm trembling because you're near me and when you're near me, I'm happy."

"I'm happy too. We're together and love is simple."

She kept smiling her lovely smile, but in her eyes Joe saw only sadness.

Joe moved into our house. With a boundless energy, he rose early to do chores, brought Claire breakfast in bed, helped her bathe, dress, and supervised her morning exercise. Only once did I hear them quarrel. My mother, breaking down and weeping, Joe disregarding her tears and urging her on.

"Once more, Claire, just one more time."

"Why do you torture me?"

"Because I love you."

"If you loved me, you wouldn't hover over every bite I eat, every step I take. You ask too much of me, Joe, and you won't face the truth: I won't walk again. All the love in the world won't give me healthy strong legs."

"Well, humor me, Claire, make me a happy man and try, once more. Just one more time."

Joe hired a woman to spend mornings with Claire. When he came home for lunch, he helped her into the wheelchair and pushed her to the office. At first she resisted. Then she began to enjoy the daily routine of helping with customers and being near Joe.

It was a small restricted world, but a world Claire was creating for herself: small currents of talk, a word on a wing, the smallest of details becoming a ritual. A morning scrub, an evening soak, my mother laughing and happy in Joe's big gentle hands.

From her wheelchair, on Sundays, she watched him work in the garden and waited for him to bring her a bouquet of flowers.

"The first moment I saw you, I fell in love, just like that, like the movies," she said. "Silly, isn't it?"

"You're silly."

"Like the movies except it's real. We're real. This moment is real."

She reached over, wiped a smudge of dirt from his face, and lifted her mouth for a kiss.

In a rare and intimate moment, Joe said, "It's not obsession, Joely, it's as if we've grown into one. One root, like a plant. When she's in pain, it's my pain too."

Did he suspect how much I loved him? Of course he did, for he said, "You're like your mother, too romantic for your own good. Be careful, Joely, these groundswells of emotion can get you into trouble."

I knew he was right but what could I do? I loved the man my mother loved. I guarded my secret, atoned, cooked the dishes Claire loved to eat, knitted for her, crocheted, any act of service or devotion to ease my sense of shame.

Six months later, Claire said to Joe, "I've been through a crisis, but this morning I awoke to a room filled with sunlight. There was a breeze, birds were singing, and I ached, Joe, ached from a happiness of being alive."

Joe took her hand and held it.

"Let me finish, darling. It's been like a bad dream, a nightmare, but it's lifted, Joe, and I saw life with a new meaning. I'm a child of Pequod. My life is here, on this island, and I'm going to photograph everything and everyone I love. I'll call it 'Claire's View from a Wheelchair.'"

"I've been dreaming of this moment."

"Not a dream, Joe. When I'm with you, nothing's a dream. Now kiss me . . . kiss me again . . . and I'm ready to go."

Claire began in the pressroom. She photographed the old machines, Joe working at his desk, the island folk coming in to report a story or linger for a moment of gossip. She wheeled herself to the wharf and took pictures of the schooners and the fishing tubs. She shot Finn's old rocker, his cigar box, a half-empty bottle of gin.

"If Finn hadn't been drinking, and I hadn't been angry, he wouldn't have gone out in the heavy rain. The gin just gave our lives an inevitability," she said.

Joe took Claire to the Seaman's Cemetery, and she photographed her mother's and father's gravestones, the toadstool growing nearby.

"I used to think I'd be buried alongside my parents, but I've changed my mind. Instead, I want you to stand on the edge of the cliff and throw my ashes into the sea, and then I want you to stand under my tree and weep."

"Aren't we being a little morbid?"

"I was morbid after the accident, but that's over, Joe. I'm not frightened anymore."

Claire shot roll upon roll of film. Pictures were printed, stacks of photographs assembled, labeled, and placed in manila folders. In the evening, Joe sat beside her and helped organize the growing piles. They argued and wrangled and discussed which photographs were best.

"My favorites are my pictures of nature, the trees and the sea," said Claire.

"No," said Joe, "the faces of Pequod are the strongest. You've caught it, Claire, the happiness, the misery, all the themes of your life. Now it's time to weave them together."

"The way you once taught me," she said, and laughed her gay sweet laugh as if she were still an imperious young island queen. She knew how it thrilled him, her laugh, her smile, and now her work; that's what she wanted, to thrill this man she had spent a lifetime in loving.

"A lifetime in loving," she told me, "and of being in thrall."

THE RAIN CONTINUED, WEEKS AND WEEKS OF SOFT, steady rain, blowing into an occasional gale. My mother was restless. "I wish it would clear up. I want to get to work." She said it every day. "I'm going to photograph my tree; married under its branches, I know its every windswept mood. I want to shoot the wind on the water and the wild, wild waves. Oh, humor me, Joe, and let me go out. I hate this confinement."

"Why can't you be sensible?"

"I wasn't born to be sensible."

"This isn't weather for anyone but a war correspondent."

"And those of us born for the wind and the rain."

Kneeling beside her, he said, "And born to be concerned. You'll get soaked, come down with a cold, or worse."

"You're not concerned, Joe, you're overconcerned. A little rain won't hurt me and all I want is an hour. Joely will drive me out but I want you to pick me up."

"Why are you so difficult?"

Claire reached over and mussed his hair.

"I know I'm difficult and I know you'll forgive me."

"I can't win, can I?"

"No, darling, you should know by now, you can't possibly win."

THE SKY HAD TURNED A DEEP GRAY AND A WIND WAS blowing up. Claire's window was open. The wind was blowing her hair. She reached out her hand to feel the rush, and pulled it back inside.

"I love it dark and ominous," she said. "As if fate's hanging over our lives. I used to be superstitious, think, foolishly, I could cheat fate. . . ."

"But how? How do you cheat fate?"

"Oh, give it a little push, a little shove to change fate's course. But when I started taking pictures, I suddenly felt safe, and that's what's so ironic; if I'd have been behind a camera instead of a steering wheel, Finn would be alive and I would be walking."

"You'll walk, Mom. Joe says you will."

"Joe's an old-fashioned optimist, and optimism is a lovely attitude, but it won't heal my back."

"It's not optimism. He honestly believes one day you'll walk."

"Remember how I used to tease you about Joe? How I called it a schoolgirl crush and said it would pass?"

"I remember."

"Well, I've come to think it was more than that."

What was Claire doing? I knew she suspected how I felt, and I wanted to tell her, to confess to my mother as she confessed to me, but I was confused and I mumbled, "Will you forgive me?"

"It's you, my Joely, who must forgive me." And dismissing the subject as she would a pesky fly, it was over, our moment of intimacy, and we drove toward the tree, Claire with her secret and me with mine.

I parked the car, helped my mother into the wheelchair, pushed it under the tree, and attached a thermos of coffee to the arm. The ground was damp from the rain, but smooth, and Claire would have the mobility to guide herself to where she wanted to go.

I looked at the sea and the long graceful slope that fell into the bay. The wind had died down and it was calm. Across the lagoon, ships and barges were tied to a wharf. I watched my mother listen to the crashing waves.

"This tree has always brought me peace," she said. "Like an oasis. That's what I want to photograph, to capture the sounds of the sea as I feel them in my heart."

And suddenly I broke down. I loved her so much. I wanted her to know, to feel my love, and I put my arm around her and put my cheek to hers, and kissed and kissed her face, and when I let her go, her eyes were shining and wet.

"Didn't I call it a tree of love? Now, one more kiss, a good-bye kiss, and let your mother go to work."

I kissed her again—I couldn't let go—and Claire raised the camera to her eye.

"You see how easy it is and how I'm not afraid."

I lingered a moment, walked to the car, and slowly drove back to the house.

THE SKY WAS DARKENING. A WIND WAS BLOWING UP, and Joe, usually at the office, was waiting at the house.

"Where's Claire? I was sure you'd bring her back."

"She wanted to stay, Joe. She was determined. Said you should pick her up in half an hour."

It was the first time I had seen him angry.

"I was a fool. I let her trick me, let that smile take me in."

He rushed out to the car and drove away.

By the time he reached the tip of the island, the wind had dropped. A pale sun was breaking through the clouds. Joe ran up to the tree but Claire wasn't there. He looked toward the bay and halfway down the slope he saw her. A stump had caught the chair by its wheel, had spun it around and overturned it. Claire's body lay crumpled on the ground. Joe rushed to her side and very gently held her.

"How handsome you are."

"Stop, Claire. I can't bear it."

"Don't frown and look angry. Please, Joe. I'm not made for more suffering."

"I'm angry with myself."

"Your arms around me, and it's like the warm sweet center of the world."

"Then why, Claire, why couldn't you hang on?"

"I tried, tried so hard, even dared to hope I was getting stronger, but I wasn't, Joe, it was a fantasy, an impossible dream—"

"Not a dream. I'm with you and you'll get stronger."

"I'm near to dying and you are raging with life."

"I'll take you home. We'll get a doctor."

"Isn't it strange how you can love someone so hard and it's suddenly over . . . kiss me . . . kiss me quickly . . . there's not much time . . ."

And all her strength seemed to pass into the kisses that now covered her face.

"I'm letting you go. . . . Let me go too . . . and take care of my Joely."

Claire's hand fell away, and Joe held her, lifeless, in his arms.

⚬⚬⚬

JOE LAID CLAIRE ON THE BED. I OPENED THE SHUTters. You could hear the stirring of leaves.

"Oh, Momma! Momma!"

There was blood on her face. Joe dampened a rag and wiped it off.

"What happened?"

"I don't know. I do know Claire was an unwilling victim in an ill-fated marriage, and I've asked myself, again and again, if my misguided loyalty to Finn didn't finally destroy them both."

"You don't mean that!"

"I mean if I had married Claire instead of agreeing to Finn's impossible scheme, they would both be alive today."

"No, Joe."

"After the accident, Claire was in constant pain. She hated being dependent, cooped up day after day, hated our pity, and was angry at dying. I don't know if Claire beat death to the draw, but I know she wanted it to look like an accident, and to that end she needed bad weather, and our assistance. That was the reason she insisted on going out today."

"What are you saying?"

"I'm saying Claire felt you were strong enough to deal with her death. It was important you drive her out, and equally important that I find her."

I remembered my mother saying, "You'll do it for me, Joely, become the honest woman I wanted to be," and suddenly, so neat and so tidy, like pieces in a puzzle, everything fit. This so-called chance accident would leave Joe free. It was Claire's gift to me, her final gift of love, every small detail thought out in advance. Oh, Mother!

Mother! So wild and romantic! Impossible! Impossible! And yet, what other reason was there for her mysterious death? Her desire to make it appear a random accident? I had to think! Had to make sense out of Claire's strange and inexplicable death.

"I'll make coffee," I said.

I went into the kitchen, put water on the stove, and filled a pot with coffee. I opened a window. A gust of wind felt good on my face. I thought of my mother, heard her say, "I should have left the island, gone away and grown up." Well, I would do it for her. I would leave Pequod and become the grown-up Claire had wanted so desperately to be.

☙❧

JOE WAS USUALLY AT THE OFFICE UNTIL AFTER DARK. When he came home we ate dinner. A few hours later he'd disappear. The house was empty and I was alone. One night it got unbearable. I knew where he had gone, so I turned on a dim porch light, got into my car, and drove to Claire's tree. I saw him standing by the cliff, silent and motionless, looking at the sea. I felt overcome. All the restraint, the feeling I had so carefully guarded these many long years, sprang up with a fury.

He heard my footsteps and turned, and in the moonlight, I saw his ravaged face, a face of utter sadness, and I knew he was calling to Claire, waiting for a sign that somehow, somewhere, she knew he was there.

"I couldn't sleep, I knew you'd be here and wouldn't mind company," I said.

"No, I'm glad you're here. I don't sleep either, and when I do I dream; I see Claire's face, I hear her voice, and for a moment she's alive. I'm awake by then, so I drive up here and I find it calms me."

"I understand."

"Do you, Joely?"

"When you love someone that hard, it's as if they're inside you."

"That last drive out," he said, changing the subject, "what did Claire talk about?"

"About fate. She said if she'd have been behind a camera instead of the wheel of a car, she would be walking and Finn would be alive."

"No, Joely, it wasn't fate. Claire was a free and independent spirit who did what she had to do to get what she wanted. She hated her dependence, foolishly worried I would one day tire of her and want to be with someone else."

"I don't think so."

"Then why, Joely? Why did she do it?"

"You'll think I'm crazy."

"Never."

I took a deep breath and began.

"Claire used to say that when her father died, her mother drowned her grief in gin. 'I never knew mother love,' she said, 'and I was desperate for it, or its substitute, and confused the love of a man with the love of a mother. Some women do that,' she said, 'women like me, who think they'll find what they yearn for in the arms of a man.' I didn't know what Claire meant, at least not then, but I'm beginning to understand. My mother knew I loved you. I think her death was a kind of heroic gesture. Claire's gift to me of mother love."

"Impossible."

"I think Claire died so you would be free."

"And I think you've inherited your mother's over-active imagination and suggest we postpone this conversation for another day. There's an all-night diner the truckers use outside of town, and I could use a cup of coffee. How about it?"

We got into our cars and drove toward the diner. I thought about my mother and her desire to get away, and I realized that leaving Pequod was not the way for me. It was Claire's idea, and Claire was Claire, and I was Joely, and I would grow up by staying where I belonged, and facing the unfinished business of Claire's and Finn's deaths.

Then I saw trucks parked outside a wood and metal structure. Joe's car was among them. I parked and went inside. Big men were eating huge servings of eggs and hash brown potatoes. Joe was sitting at the counter. I sat beside him in an empty chair.

"Hungry?"

"Coffee's fine."

He ordered two coffees.

"Joe?"

"Yes, Joely."

"My mother used to say she would have grown up if she had left the island and gone into the world, but I know a ferry ride across the bay isn't going to turn me into a woman."

"You're right, Joely. Your life is here, on Pequod." He paused. "I'll go instead. It's the wisest thing I can do. I'll use Boston as a base and I'm an hour away if you need me. That's what you want, isn't it?"

"Yes. It's what I want."

He pulled a wallet from a pocket and paid the bill. Outside, the sky was streaked with light.

"You've grown up with the presses and the smell of printer's ink. We'll hire some experienced help and I know you'll be okay."

"Yes, I'll be okay."

"It'll take a few days to get my things in order. Right now I'm exhausted and all I want is a few hours' sleep."

I watched him drive away and wondered why I'd told him. It was a silly question. I'd told him because I wanted him to know.

❧

JOE IS LEAVING TOMORROW.

He wanted to sleep alone tonight, said it would be

easier. As for me, I hardly slept. This strange obsession torments me. Yes, I love him, or is it my mother's love I seek, Claire in his kisses, my mother through Joe?

A door connects our rooms and through a crack I hear him breathe. Soon it will be dawn. I can stand it no longer and go into his room. He is sleeping, or pretending. I slide between the sheets and touch his shoulder. I kiss it. He raises himself and looks into my eyes.

"Don't you see what you're doing, Joely? You're using sex to blot out death, and sex is not the answer. It will leave you confused and conflicted, so I am banishing you to your room."

"In a minute."

"I'm leaving tomorrow and your life will be simple. Now get the hell out of my bed."

I watched him walk up the ramp and board the ferry. He waved from the deck and I waved back and whispered, "Thank you for pushing me into some sort of self-respect." The ferry sailed away, and I knew it had begun, the first baby steps of growing into the woman Claire would have wanted me to be.

I T WAS A BLEAK AND DREARY WINTER, THE SOUNDS OF life locked beneath the surface of the earth, or bolted behind farmhouse doors. A world of gray sky and sea and barren field. Flumes of smoke rose from chimneys, gale-force winds pounded the houses, torrential rains flooded the ground.

And suddenly, tulips, daffodils, and shimmering dogwood covered the island. It was spring and everyone rushed outside. Neighbor greeted neighbor, church bells rang, schooners creaked, and car horns honked as Pequod prepared for the hustle and rush of the summer crowds.

I didn't call Joe while he was away but every week he checked in. When he saw I could manage without his help, he said he was hard at work and would not return until he had finished his book.

A year has passed. I push the thought of Joe away, and life is easier. I wake up early, throw myself into the daily problems that are a part of publishing a weekly news-paper, eat dinner at a nearby restaurant, come home, and fall exhausted into bed.

CRSD

I SEE A FERRY IN THE DISTANCE, THE BOAT BRINGING him home, and then it docks, and one by one the passengers disembark. Joe walks down the ramp and I watch that long, rangy stride, and it is as if lightning has struck in the same spot.

And now he stands beside me, his hand on my shoulder, his lips on my cheek, and it's like someone has banged me on the chest and my ribs have collapsed.

"Congratulations! You've kept the *Post* alive and kicking."

"I've tried my damnedest."

"And grown up, too!"

"You cannot imagine how much!"

He throws back his head and laughs and it is useless to struggle. I've always loved him, perhaps I always will.

He pulls a suitcase from the gurney and we get into my car, pass the weather-beaten statue of a sailor lost at sea, boatyards and oil refineries, wooden piers on pebbled beaches, shacks standing strong after the winter winds, and Joe is silent.

I had longed to see him, days and nights of longing, and now, beside me, we drive along in silence.

"What are you thinking?" I say.

"I'm thinking I'm old enough to be your father, though I don't imagine something as simple as age is going to stand in your way."

"Is that a proposal?"

"And another thing, I've got work to do and can't be with some love-besotted creature who will give me no privacy or peace."

"It is a proposal. You're asking me to marry you."

"And last, but certainly not least, I feel as if I've climbed a very high mountain, an emotional Everest, and I want a quiet normal life. Do you think we can manage a day-by-day normal existence?"

"I want it too, a normal life. What I don't want is to be married at dawn under a tree with the sound of waves pounding the rocks. I don't want a tangled wreck of a life, or the kind of passion that pulled my mother to her death, and I wonder, yes, I wonder is it Claire you love, or is it Claire, through me?"

I glance at him, somber in profile, but in that instant I know.

"My love for you has nothing to do with my loving Claire."

"Except you'll look in my eyes and see her, you'll hold me in your arms and think of her, my mother's lover will hold and kiss me. My mother is still with us as if she was alive."

I park in front of his house. The sun has come out. He pulls his suitcase from the backseat and leans on the open front window. He reaches his hand toward mine.

"You're your mother's daughter, even more than you can imagine."

He pulls away his hand and walks back alone to his house.

SOON IT WILL BE DAWN. THE SUN WILL HIT THE TREES and fall onto the cobbled streets. You can hear the motors of the quahog boats, the clink of bottles as the milkman makes his rounds, the blast of the ferry, bringing life to the island or taking it away. The *Pequod Post* will begin a new day. A customer will place an ad, a notice of a church meeting, a birth, wedding, or death, and we will run an editorial on some hot issue splitting the island. The old presses will sputter and spin, nothing big or dramatic, but life will seem normal.

And on a Sunday afternoon, I will drive to the cliffs and under Claire's tree I will look at the sea and remember my mother, my passionate mother, who looks down on me and smiles.

ABOUT THE AUTHOR

JUDY FEIFFER was raised in Italy and California. She worked on a French fashion magazine and then, in New York, became a photographer. She has been a production executive with Warner Bros. and Orion Pictures, as well as a senior editor at William Morrow. Ms. Feiffer is the author of three previous novels, *A Hot Property, Lovecrazy,* and *Flame.* She has a daughter, Kate, and lives in New York.

ABOUT THE TYPE

This book was set in Granjon, a modern recutting of a typeface produced under the direction of George W. Jones, who based Granjon's design upon the letterforms of Claude Garamond (1480–1561). The name was given to the typeface as a tribute to the typographic designer Robert Granjon.